***The best, the absolute wisest thing
Lilah could do for herself would be to
stay away.***

She had a life—two lives—to put back in order.
And standing so close to him now, thinking
things she prayed her face would not reveal,
Lilah felt a traitorous bloom of red creep up her
neck.

"I'm planning a large party in September," he
said smoothly. "If you're here in the fall, be sure
to drop by and help us celebrate."

Say something, a voice inside her urged. "What
will you be celebrating?"

A satisfied smile crawled leisurely, easily across
Gus's handsome face. He looked every inch the
contented man, every inch the success, proof that
America was still the land of self-made men and
second chances. "My marriage."

Y0-BRA-319

Dear Reader,

Several years ago, my husband planned our first road trip. For a week we visited the graves of every outlaw who had died between Oregon and North Dakota. By the time we reached Deadwood, I threatened to fly home. I'm glad I didn't, because in North Dakota, we stayed in a tiny, delightful town surrounded by fields of wild mustard, acres of whispering barley and choke cherries that showed up in everything, including pies, preserves and candies. The people were kind and idiosyncratic and wonderful. I began my book, *Dakota Bride,* on the drive home. In *Once More, At Midnight* I revisit the town of Kalamoose and the Owens sisters, Nettie, Sara and Lilah. It's Lilah's turn to fall in love. I hope you'll have as much fun in Kalamoose as I do. By the way, if you ever drive from Oregon to North Dakota, skip the graves and see the Tetons!

Wendy Warren

ONCE MORE, AT MIDNIGHT

WENDY WARREN

SPECIAL EDITION

Published by Silhouette Books

America's Publisher of Contemporary Romance

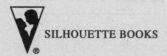

SILHOUETTE BOOKS

ISBN-13: 978-0-373-24817-9
ISBN-10: 0-373-24817-2

ONCE MORE, AT MIDNIGHT

Books by Wendy Warren

Silhouette Special Edition

Dakota Bride #1463
Making Babies #1644
Undercover Nanny #1710
*The Boss and Miss Baxter #1737
One More, At Miidnight #1817

*Family Business

Silhouette Romance

Mr. Wright #936
Romantics Anonymous #981
Oh, Baby! #1033
Her Very Own Husband #1148
Just Say I Do #1236
The Drifter's Gift #1268
The Oldest Virgin in Oakdale #1609

WENDY WARREN

lives with her husband and daughter in the beautiful Pacific Northwest. Their house was previously owned by a woman named Cinderella, who bequeathed them a garden full of flowers they try desperately (and occasionally successfully) not to kill, and a pink General Electric oven, circa 1958, that makes the kitchen look like an *I Love Lucy* rerun.

A two-time recipient of the Romance Writers of America's RITA® Award, Wendy loves to read and write the kind of books that remind her of the old movies she grew up watching with her mom—stories about decent people looking for the love that can make an ordinary life heroic. When not writing, she likes to take long walks, hide out in bookstores with her friends and sneak tofu into her husband's dinner. If you'd like a tofu recipe—and who wouldn't—visit her at www.wendywarren-author.com.

In memory of Chauncie Bella,
my sweet, sweet dog. Thank you for fourteen
love-filled years and for showing me it is possible
never to have an unkind moment. Walks won't be
the same without you, wonderful friend.

My thanks and love to the friends, old and new,
whose presence and care helped so much during
Chauncie's illness—Lainee, Cathy, Denise and Dan,
Maggie, Rob and Jen, and the staffs of Powell Blvd.
Veterinary Clinic, Housecalls for Pets and
Dove Lewis. There are angels everywhere.

Chapter One

"It's-too-hot-This-place-smells-I'm-hungry-I-have-to-pee-You-drive-too-slow."

It's incredible, Lilah Owens thought, fingers curling around the steering wheel of her old Pontiac. *The kid can complain without punctuation.*

She looked at her passenger, trying to be patient, because the eleven-year-old had been through a lot in the past several weeks.

Then again, so had Lilah. That, coupled with the fact that she was also hot, hungry and had to pee, tended to blunt her compassion. She took a deep breath, as deep as if she were about to belt a song, and answered back, "If-you're-so-hot-suck-on-some-ice-We-just-drove-past-a-sheep-ranch-so-what-do-you-expect-You-ate-an-entire-bag-of-Funyuns-five-minutes-ago-You-can-pee-when-we-get-where-we're-going-And-this-car-is-moving-as-fast-as-she-can-If-you-don't-like-it-get-out-and-walk."

She felt fairly pleased with herself until her passenger's small fingers reached for the door handle and tugged. True to form, her stubborn Sunfire did not give in easily. Eventually, though, the rusty car relented and the door swung open. On the highway. At the Pontiac's top speed of forty miles per hour.

"Are you crazy?!" Lilah lunged across Sabrina's thankfully seat-belted body to grab for the door. She caught the handle on the first try, pulled with all her might and managed to shut them in tight again, locking the door for good measure. *"Never do that again,"* she said, glaring at Bree with fury and disbelief. "Do you want to get us killed?"

Bree shrugged with apparent lack of concern.

Lilah tried to breathe past the pounding of her heart and wondered, not for the first time, if they would actually survive this road trip. The tension had mounted with each mile they'd traveled from California to North Dakota.

Looking out the windshield, she dropped her usual cynicism and for a moment allowed herself to imagine there was a heaven somewhere behind the blindingly hot summer sun.

I know, I promised to act like a mother, Gracie....

Silently, Lilah spoke to the friend who had passed on a month earlier and, who, if there was a heaven, certainly deserved to be there. *But I may kick Sabrina out of the car myself.*

Grace McKuen had been a perfect friend. Perfect in every way, except in her estimation of Lilah's ability to take care of a child. Four months ago, Grace had discovered that her body was rejecting her second kidney transplant. A month later she and her daughter, Sabrina, had moved in with Lilah. Two months after that, Gracie was gone, and Lilah Owens, singleton, had become, Lilah Owens, instant mother. Add hot water and stir. Now she knew what she'd merely guessed at before: motherhood was only slightly less daunting than skydiving without a parachute.

"I saw a sign that said 'gas and food, two miles,'" Bree insisted, still using the tone of voice that made Lilah want to open the door and step out of the car herself. "That was probably a mile and ninety-nine one hundredths ago, so like it would kill you to think of *someone else for five seconds?*"

Lilah brought a smile—the sweetest one she could muster—to her face. Perhaps if she pretended she was Florence Henderson on *The Brady Bunch* she could respond without doing Bree harm. "I told you, Sabrina—" *you little pisher* "—I lived in this area for seventeen years. The only gas station on this road closed in 1989. So, you'll have to wait until—"

"Oh, big wow, you lived here seventeen years," Bree

interrupted. "You're *way* older since then. They could have built, like, a nuclear sub station by now."

"So," Lilah continued, "you may have misread the sign."

"As *i-i-i-f.* If I misread the sign, what's that?" She pointed, and Lilah followed the direction of the skinny arm, mostly so she wouldn't have to make eye contact.

She squinted.

Ohmigod.

On their side of the quiet two-lane highway, no more than fifty yards ahead, was a large sign that read Union Gas and Minimart. A gas station *and* a minimart? Lilah gaped. On a highway that led to a string of towns so small and insignificant they hadn't appeared on a map since Custer whupped Sitting Bull?

She shook her head. Well, crud. Now she would have to deal with a rude, angry, *right* preteen. "Okay. We'll stop for a bathroom break," she conceded, adding in a mutter, "I can't believe someone put a minimart out here. Everything will go stale inside of a year."

"Maybe they sell food to kids whose guardians *aren't* trying to starve and torture them. I have to *pee-ee!*"

Gritting her teeth, Lilah pressed the accelerator. Even though her own bladder was crying for relief, she would have kept going if it were up to her. Her sister's house was perhaps a half hour down the road, and Lilah wanted to get there soon.

Now.

Yesterday.

More than a potty break, she needed the comfort of sisterly arms, a commiserating smile and someone who knew her well enough to understand that unexpected motherhood had thrown her into a panic worthy of a Valium drip.

Turning into a station that boasted two bays of shiny new pumps, Lilah pulled alongside a handsome structure designed to resemble an old-fashioned general market. The minimart had a wood exterior and a window painted in block letters that read Free Ice Water and Restrooms Inside.

Parking, she attempted a tone of good cheer, as if stopping had been her idea all along. There had to be some way to get along with an angry eleven-year-old. "So, okay! Let's check out that bathroom and then—"

Bree was out of the car and pushing open the store's glass door before Lilah could unbuckle her seat belt. Sighing, she hauled her stiff body out of the car feeling still more defeated. *Note to self: Save tone of good cheer for someone who gives a flip.*

She grabbed her purse, shaking off the food wrappers Bree had thrown into the backseat despite the plastic bag Lilah had given her for garbage. Carrying what she could, she dumped the empty bags and drink containers into a trash can at the front of the store.

Lilah had spent the past decade in Los Angeles going on acting auditions and waiting tables while she hoped for the big break that still hadn't come. In retrospect it was excellent preparation for motherhood; God knew she was used to rejection and feelings of inadequacy. Even so, those years in L.A. were a piece of cake compared to the past month with Bree.

Shoving her sunglasses atop blond hair that, sadly, had not seen a stylist in six months, Lilah followed her charge into the store then blinked in surprise at the attractive and well-stocked market.

A young woman she recognized immediately as Lakota Indian sat on a stool behind the counter. "Hi," the girl greeted, white teeth gleaming in contrast to her dark skin and hair. "Do you need gas?"

"No, thanks," Lilah declined, noting that Bree was already disappearing into the restroom at the rear of the store. Since that appeared to be the only women's restroom, Lilah hovered by the cashier. Lord, she was tired.

"The cookies are fresh if you're hungry, and we have iced lattes."

Lilah looked at the girl, who pointed to a highly polished cappuccino machine. A drink menu sat on the counter. She didn't want to be rude, but she felt her first genuine chuckle in weeks coming on. *Iced lattes? In Kalamoose?*

Born and raised just a few miles from here, Lilah considered her hometown to be a dead ringer for Mayberry, R.F.D., except that Mayberry was more hip. As far as she'd been able to tell on her infrequent visits home, the only thing that had changed in Kalamoose in the dozen and a half years since she'd made her escape were the heads of lettuce at Hertzog's Grocery, and rumor had it that a few of those were still the originals.

Now someone had opened a gas station that served lattes? That someone was a little out of the loop.

Passing on the coffee drink, Lilah ventured, "Your sign mentioned ice water?"

Apparently unfazed that her only customers had stopped in to use the john and bum a free beverage, the clerk nodded pleasantly. "All the way in the back. Cups are next to the cooler. Help yourself."

Lilah reached the water as Bree emerged from the restroom.

"Do they have hot dogs?" the girl asked before she'd truly acknowledged Lilah's presence.

"I don't think so."

"Well, then I want a Coke."

"Negative, Commander. You've had so much sugar and caffeine on this trip you could have flown to North Dakota." When Bree looked like she was about to protest—loudly—Lilah decided she'd had enough. Pointing, she said, "There's a water cooler right there. Have all the ice water you can hold, but don't start with me. My sister Nettie is a fabulous cook. You can drink and gorge yourself into a stupor after we arrive, but from now until then no more anything."

"I'm gonna look at the magazines." Shrugging as if the matter was no longer of any interest to her, Bree put her hands in the pockets of her low-slung jeans and slouched off.

Lilah sighed heavily and downed a cup of water, wishing it were a stiff tequila. She ducked briefly into the restroom and emerged to discover Bree in the candy aisle, about to shoplift a Carmello bar.

"Stop!" Hissing, Lilah grabbed the candy the girl had been about to tuck into the waistband of her jeans, beneath her T-shirt. "What do you think you're doing? Now you're a thief? What is the matter with you?"

Careful not to crush the candy bar in her tensed fist, Lilah closed her eyes and tried to collect herself. *She's only eleven. She just lost the only mother she's ever known. She's acting out. The only cool you can keep is your own.*

"Bree." Lilah began again by greatly modifying her tone. She looked directly into the rebellious hazel eyes. "Grace…your mother…was the most honest woman I've ever met. She wanted nothing but the best for you. How do you think she'd feel if she saw you trying to shoplift?"

Bree shrugged with classic impenetrable sedition. "Not as bad as she'd feel if she knew you wouldn't buy it for me."

The last of Lilah's anger deflated like a popped balloon. With no job, she'd been trying to carefully budget their cash. Yesterday she had limited the between-meal treats to three a day. Today, at Bree's insistence that she was going through a growth spurt and needed extra calories, Lilah had amended the limit to six. She didn't know what was right anymore.

"Look, Bree…" Clutching the candy bar in a death

grip, she took a stab at reason and compassion. "I know this is a really, really difficult time for you. I wasn't much older than you are now when my mother died. It's awful, and it's probably not going to get a whole lot better right away. At least, it didn't for me. But if you could just give me a chance here, I bet you and I…you know…I bet we could be friends."

Bree rolled her eyes. Frustration rocketed up Lilah's body. Maybe she ought to buy the candy. Maybe she ought to buy a lot of candy and eat most of it herself.

Suddenly she noticed a bulge in Bree's pocket, a bulge that had not been there before. Disappointment sucked her heart to the pit of her stomach.

"Did you take anything besides the Carmello?"

Bree responded with a stone-faced stare.

Lilah raised both hands. "Cut me a break! One of my sisters is the sheriff of Kalamoose. She will freak if she hears you picked up a rock from the playground without asking, much less that you tried to pinch half the chocolate in town." Bree remained impassive. "My sister, Sara, is very, very scary."

Following a prolonged stare down, which resulted in absolutely nothing, Lilah held out her hand. "Give me whatever is in your pocket. Please." Her request was met with crossed arms and a bite-me glare. Instantly, Lilah realized she had to win this battle or risk losing the war.

Trying not to attract the clerk's notice, she moved quickly toward Bree, ending up in a brief wrestling match until she was able to pull a Baby Ruth, a packet of M&M's and a box of Junior Mints from the girl's baggy pants pocket. Torn between triumph and dismay, she was about to return the candy to its proper place when Bree took off.

Lilah followed, but Bree was faster, and the element of surprise was on her side. Lilah hadn't made it past the chips before Bree was through the door. Throwing her entire body into the effort to catch up, Lilah ran smack into a barrier at the end of the aisle.

"Oof!" She grabbed him to steady herself.

Big, steel-vise hands gripped her shoulders as she rebounded off the chest of a man who stood a good six inches taller than her own five foot eight. Beautifully cut from exquisite material, the suit she clutched to keep herself upright was as out of place in a North Dakota minimart as the Hope diamond in a box of Cracker Jack. Catching a whiff of expensive cologne, Lilah looked up, a hasty apology ready on her lips.

It died the moment she saw his face.

No. Way.

Winter-gray eyes scanned her without betraying a flicker of the surprise he must have felt. Recognition, but not pleasure, lent a curve to his lips.

"Leaving so soon?"

The timbre of his voice had remained the same, though his diction emerged more crisply than she recalled.

Gus Hoffman.

It had been a dozen years since they'd stood face-to-face. Lilah had been only seventeen then, but Gus had

mimicked. "Jeez, Gus, you're making a big deal out of nothing. I know this situation looks a little funny, but you of all people ought to understand mistaken impressions. Bree was running to the car to get her money, because I said I wouldn't buy any more sugar," she fibbed. She raised her hands. "That's it. No biggie."

The glass door opened, and Bree entered, steered by Gus's employee. The eleven-year-old looked belligerent but worried and frightened, too, when she made eye contact with Lilah, as if she feared her guardian had ratted her out.

Lilah felt the stirrings of real compassion, along with a rumble of nerves that made her queasy. Bree's sandy blond hair was mussed from the car ride, her clothes were wrinkled and spotted with food stains and she looked plain miserable. Anyone taking note of her would be sure to have questions for Lilah, beginning with "What are *you* doing with a kid?"

The last thing Lilah wanted to do right now was answer questions about Bree. Or about what she'd done with her life the past twelve years. The second to last thing she wanted to do was let Gus Hoffman intimidate her in front of Bree.

With the single goal of getting back in her car and on the road uppermost in her mind, Lilah raised the broken, not to mention sweaty, candy bar in her hand. "You know, I think I will buy this. There are so many studies now about the benefits of chocolate, who am I to argue with scientific evidence?"

She looked over Gus's shoulder, to where Sabrina was standing very still. "Never mind about raiding your piggy bank, honey. Auntie Lilah will buy the snacks."

From the corner of her eye, she watched Gus's expression subtly register the term *auntie*. Reaching toward a rack, she snagged a large bag of baked potato chips and forced herself to casually study the ingredients. "Hmm. Low in fat and full of potassium. We'll take these, too." She smiled. "Come on, Bree."

The moment she stepped past Gus, she shot Bree a look that said, *Do not screw with me now.*

Willing at last to follow Lilah's lead, the child nodded.

Commanding herself to stand tall, to walk as if she'd spent the past four days shopping in Neiman Marcus rather than riding in a sweltering car while she panicked about the complicated quagmire her life had become, Lilah headed to the cash register.

It had long been her habit to bolster her self-confidence by tending to every detail of her appearance. Now she was acutely aware that her makeup had melted in the heat, her khaki shorts and sleeveless white top were wrinkled from the long drive and she hadn't had a manicure in months and months.

She recalled the first time she'd met Gus. Only ten, she'd already started dressing to mimic the current month's cover of *Seventeen* magazine. Gus, on the other hand, had looked like he worked on a farm and hadn't changed his clothes in a week. Streaked with dirt and smelling like sheep, he'd covered his dirty body with ripped pants and a T-shirt that was stained, too large and nearly worn through in spots.

How times had changed.

There were so many things she could have asked him: *How've you been? How did the boy I knew turn into the man standing before me? Have you ever considered forgiving me?*

She kept quiet, feeling his gaze spear her back as she placed the food on the counter then fished loose change from the bottom of her purse. She expected the clerk to resume her place, but instead Gus strode to the register, rang up the candy bar and chips and took the money she set down. He dropped her purchases and the receipt into a paper bag and handed them to her. He never took his eyes off her, and he never smiled. The stern angles of his face and sculpted jaw betrayed the Lakota half of his heritage. Clear gray eyes and hair the color of maple sugar, both bequeathed by his German ancestors, might have softened his looks, if not for the stark mistrust in his expression.

Lilah was beyond careful when she took the bag. She didn't want to so much as graze his pinky. She just wanted to get out of there.

Backing away from the counter, she made the mistake of looking up and saw that Gus had transferred his gaze briefly to Bree. He looked at the girl then back at Lilah and his stare was assessing.

The horrible nerves that seemed never to leave her now kicked into overdrive. *Run, run, run,* they warned, but Lilah had never been good with exits, and sure enough she began to muck up this one.

"Well, Nettie is waiting for us, and we're running late as it is." She kept moving toward Bree, but the silence intimidated her. "The store looks great," she offered in parting. "Good candy selection. And lattes—that's what I call one-stop shopping. Best of luck."

Slinging her purse over her shoulder, she grabbed Bree's skinny arm and dragged her out the door.

"What's wrong with you?" the girl mumbled as Lilah hauled her to the car.

"Buckle your seat belt." Jamming the key in the ignition and resisting a worried glance in the rearview mirror, Lilah peeled away from the station as fast as she could.

"Are you always so mental around guys?"

Leaning as far over her knees as her seat belt would allow, Bree gaped at Lilah. "You were, like, practically a retard in there."

"Don't say 'retard.'" Lilah glanced from her passenger to the speedometer and consciously slowed her aging vehicle. Not that the car could ever *speed,* but Lilah was shaking so badly she feared a strong breeze could wrest the wheel from her hands. "That's horribly rude."

"Okay. I can't believe I'm going to spend my formative years with someone who acts like a dork. How am I supposed to learn anything?" Bree complained with classic adolescent drama, but for the first time in ages, she seemed almost cheerful.

If you learn anything from me at all, learn from my mistakes, Lilah wanted to say, but didn't. Craving freedom from conversation, she put a tape of Broadway melodies in the cassette player.

Bree listened to the music for a full two seconds then asked, "Are you always so mental around guys?"

Lilah gritted her teeth. "Yes."

"Oh." Bree scratched at a scab on her elbow. "Me, too." Punching the eject button on the stereo, she pulled out the Broadway tape and replaced it with Coldplay.

Lilah glanced over. At another time she would have followed the thread of this conversation, used it to establish rapport with Bree, but right now it simply wasn't in her. Even though they were headed away from Gus, Lilah's stomach rumbled so violently she thought she might have to stop the car.

Why hadn't one of her sisters mentioned that Gus had returned? As the owner of a brand-new gas station, Gus must have been in town a while, and no one had said a word to her.

Wiping her brow, Lilah tried to comfort herself with the supposition that if her sisters hadn't mentioned Gus then perhaps they didn't remember that she had once been hot and heavy with the least-likely-to-succeed boy in all of Kalamoose county. At that thought, she felt her stomach unclench a little.

If they hadn't mentioned Gus then clearly they didn't suspect she'd left town in part to get away from him.

And, if her sisters had not mentioned Gus's return—

in a designer suit—then surely they had no idea that when he'd been escorted from Kalamoose twelve years ago—in handcuffs—Lilah had been at least partly responsible for the act that had sent him to prison.

Chapter Two

If a man wore a suit in the middle of summer it was either because his job compelled him to or because he trusted himself not to sweat.

Gus Hoffman could wear anything he wanted to work; he was his own boss. He wore the suit because it commanded respect, because it said that he was serious about his business and his place in the community, and because these days he didn't sweat unless he was working out.

He had learned to use his mind to govern his body, his actions and his reactions. He'd learned the powerful art of self-control.

Lilah Owens had just shot that to hell.

Tension made Gus's voice tight as he spoke to the young woman he'd hired to manage his store. "The daily audits look good, Crystal. I'll stop in again tomorrow. Call if you need anything before then."

Crystal nodded. Following his lead, she said nothing about the incident that had just occurred.

"We'll be fine here." Crystal was composed by nature, and she was Lakota; she read Gus well enough to know when to converse and when not to.

With a nod in return, he left the minimart. Squinting in the sun, he walked around the building to the open garage, where he'd parked his car, and raised a hand in acknowledgement to Crystal's cousin Jim, also Lakota, who toiled over the clutch of a Ford pickup and worked the pumps.

The gas station was pulling a decent business in gas and repair work and more business would be coming Gus's way; he was certain of it. He liked risks, but he didn't gamble unnecessarily. He'd come back to North Dakota with plans, not only for the station, but for Kalamoose.

Twelve years ago he'd left town with his head hung low, carrying shame and frustration that had dogged him most of his life. He'd owned nothing, had dropped out of school and alienated anyone who might have helped him.

And he'd left town hating Lilah Owens the same way he'd loved her—ferociously, blindly, passionately.

Starting the engine of a Lexus SC, he put the convertible in Reverse, pulled out of the garage and jammed on a pair of hundred-and-fifty-dollar sunglasses to block the glare.

The shock on Lilah's face when she'd realized he *owned* the gas station had filled him with satisfaction—and churning resentment. She hadn't expected him to amount to crap, had she?

Gunning the car's engine, Gus headed for the highway, toward nowhere in particular.

It had been a long while since he'd craved danger and speed; apparently Lilah still had a deleterious affect on his judgment. He wouldn't allow himself to think about her for long.

He had learned to manage his thoughts the way he managed his businesses: by allotting time only to that which would bring success and by turning away from distractions.

Starting his mental clock, he decided to allot Lilah two minutes. That would be enough time to assess his feelings.

First, he reminded himself that seeing her again should have come as no surprise, no jolt at all. When he'd returned to Kalamoose, he had accepted as fact that she would be back to visit her sisters some day and that he might run into her. He'd looked forward to the meeting, to showing her he'd moved on—and up—without her love, without her support, without any of the things he'd once believed he needed in order to breathe.

He could live, he'd since learned, without a lot of things. And Lilah Owens was one of them.

Thirty seconds down; a minute and a half to go....

He briefly allowed himself to relive that first moment of seeing her again. She'd been wrestling with a kid who was obviously shoplifting. He could have stepped in—he'd just exited his office when the tussle began—but he'd hung back, taken the opportunity to let his revved senses calm and to study the woman he'd known he would see again one day. Without the perfectly chosen, perfectly pressed clothes she had once favored, without the makeup, without the soft teenage perfection, Lilah was still—

He swore and pressed the gas pedal.

The golden girl of Kal High was still built like every man's fantasy. She looked tired, as if she hadn't slept well, but she still had cat eyes—golden-green and blazing—and lips full enough to make most men eschew common sense.

Easing off the pedal when the speedometer hit eighty-five, Gus wondered about the kid. He knew nothing about children, but guessed the girl to be a young teen, or nearly so. She was tall, belligerent and looked a little like Lilah's older sister, Sara, with whom Gus had never hit it off. Could be Sara's kid, he supposed, or maybe the younger one's—Nettie's. He'd heard she'd married and lived part time in Kalamoose, part time in New York. Beyond that meager information about the Owenses, he had studiously avoided all gossip.

He'd already dismissed the likelihood that the girl was Lilah's daughter. The tussle over the candy had been awkward, as if they weren't used to touching. There was no familial spark.

Another thirty seconds down. *Don't waste any more time on the kid.*

For his last minute of reflection on Lilah Owens, Gus decided to remember the most important part of their relationship: She had betrayed him. In one unforgettable moment she had cut out the heart he had discovered only by loving her.

For a long, long time, Gus had wished a similar pain befell her. He'd hoped she would fall in love, learn to trust and let herself need someone who would throw it all back in her face.

For a long time, hatred had kept him alive but stupid. He'd made piss-poor choices and asinine mistakes.

Finally he'd realized hatred held a person in the gutter, but that righteous fury could be a powerful motivator. That's when he began to fight the right way.

He'd battled for opportunities he'd never have hoped for in the past. He'd swallowed his pride—and his arrogance—and worked with integrity when he thought a menial task would lead to something more. He learned how to conform, or at least to give the appearance of doing so when it would benefit him. He'd sought mentors and when they'd advised him, he'd listened.

Over the years, Gus had become more than anyone had ever imagined he would be. More, even, than he'd dared hope to become.

His passion had served him. And once it had, he'd let it go.

Somewhere along the line, he'd stopped picturing Lilah with every job he'd taken, every bank account he'd opened. There had come a time when he'd tried on a thousand-dollar suit and sought his own approval, not hers, in the mirror. In that moment he had known that he was ready to move on personally, not just professionally. He'd finally been able to start living and would eventually try his hand at loving. He'd moved past caring what Lilah Owens felt or thought about, or whether she'd ever regretted her actions....

Until fifteen minutes ago.

"Let me get this straight: The kid's mother gives you—a woman she hasn't seen in years—custody of her kid, and you have no choice in the matter?"

Seated behind her broad oak desk, dressed in her sheriff's uniform, red hair slicked back into an honest-to-God, old-fashioned bun, Sara Owens looked and sounded more like a suspicious law enforcement agent than the warm, supportive sister Lilah needed right now.

"Keep your voice down," Lilah cautioned, glancing to the jail cells Bree was presently investigating. At least the fact that Sara worked in a jail had scored points with the chronically unimpressed preteen. Sara had given her permission to nose around and that bought Lilah a few minutes to try to explain her current situation to her sister. "Of course I had a choice in the matter. You can't force someone to take a child."

"So?" Sara raised her hands. "Why do you still have her?"

Glancing toward the cells, Lilah wondered which

details to relay and which to leave out. She hadn't had the chutzpah to tell anyone the *whole* story. Not yet.

"I'm going to raise her."

Sara put her head in her hands.

Lilah's stomach burned. This was why she had been hoping to tell Nettie first. Nettie was gentle. Nettie was polite. Nettie was the youngest sister, but among the three of them she was the only one who had ever possessed a modicum of maternal instincts. When their parents died, it had been Nettie who'd assumed the role of nurturer and caretaker. Although Lilah and Sara were older and should have been the ones taking care of their baby sis, they had learned to rely on Nettie for their emotional needs, for reminders to complete their homework and for edible meals. Looking back, they had taken her for granted.

After driving across several states with Bree and then seeing Gus Hoffman, Lilah needed Nettie's comfort and her levelheaded advice more than ever. She'd driven straight to Nettie's from the gas station, but the house had been locked up tight. On her own, Lilah would have stayed put and waited. Bree, on the other hand, had started complaining about the heat and the threat of starvation, so Lilah had reluctantly come to the sheriff's station.

Standing before Sara's narrowed green eyes and their eagle-sharp scrutiny made Lilah remember why she'd rarely trusted Sara with her secrets, even when they were both kids. Sara's world was black and white. Actions were either right or wrong, good or bad; you did something or you didn't do it—case closed, end of story, next case. Lilah had never understood that.

Picking her way carefully over the rocky terrain of explanations, she attempted to answer Sara without provoking a cross-examination.

"Grace was my best friend when I first got to L.A. She was the receptionist at the first acting agency I signed with, and she took me under her wing and told me who I could trust and who to steer clear from. She saved my butt lots of times. I owed her any help I could give her."

Sara squinted as if she were in pain. It made her look like Robert De Niro. "She helped you with your acting stuff, so you think you should take her kid?"

Lilah told herself not to get defensive, but she was exhausted and couldn't stop thinking about Gus—two conditions guaranteed to put her on edge. And the way Sara said "your acting stuff" reminded her that in her older sister's eyes she'd failed in just about every area of her life.

"I'm not going to let Sabrina down," she said, "and you know what? You're not going to understand this, so just drop it, Sara."

Sara leaned over her desk, cheeks turning as red as her hair. "I'm not going to understand it? Why?" She splayed a big-boned hand on her chest. "Are you implying that *I* would let someone down? That I'm not reliable?"

"Geesh, Sara, no—"

"I sure as hell hope not, because as I recall I'm not the one who moved fifteen hundred miles from my family so I could be on the *New Dating Game*."

"Oh, that's it!" Lilah stood and knocked over a half-dead aloe vera plant as she swung her purse onto her shoulder. "Do you have Nettie's cell number?"

"What for?"

"Because I'm hungry, and I want her recipe for bread pudding." Lilah reached for the phone on Sara's desk and held it up, waiting for the number. "She wasn't home, and I would like to see a *friendly* face after driving across half the country, so just give me the number."

Sara rose, too, stabbing her index finger into her own chest. "I'm friendly. I'm one of the friendliest damned people you'll ever meet."

"That's right. Ask anyone." A rough voice and booted footsteps forestalled a comment from Lilah, who turned to see that Nick Brady, a farmer with property that adjoined Sara's land, had entered the jail. He walked toward them with an ironic quirk on his handsome lips and a lazy roll in his gait.

Lilah would have greeted her old girlhood neighbor if Sara hadn't grumbled, "Don't you ever knock?"

"To enter a public building? Not often." Nick's half-hooded eyes mocked her ungently. "Besides, you're so friendly." He turned to Lilah and offered a smile. "Good to see you back home. You're as beautiful as ever."

She wasn't, but Lilah knew the comment was intended more to infuriate Sara than to compliment the recipient, so she smiled. "I can always count on your charm to see past my flaws, Nick. How've you been?" They shared a brief embrace.

"Fine as always." He nodded toward one of the open cells on the other side of the small, old-fashioned jailhouse. "I see you've got company."

"That's Bree," Lilah said. "She's with me."

Nick, being Nick, did not press for more information. He simply nodded. "You planning to be in town awhile?"

"Indefinitely."

Sara's auburn brows jacked up.

Taking a moment to eyeball his old nemesis and her shocked expression, Nick commented to Lilah, "Chase had to go to New York on business, so Nettie took Colin to see the sights. I assume she didn't know you'd be here, or she'd never have left. I suppose that means you're staying at Sara's?"

The sisters looked at each other with expressions approaching horror. Sara lived in their old family home, and Lilah had stayed there for brief visits, but always with Nettie present to run interference.

"How long will Chase and Nettie be gone?" she asked weakly.

Nick rolled his large shoulders. "Hard to say. Chase told me he wants to surprise Colin with a trip to Disney World. 'Course, you know Nettie. If she knows you're here, she'll hightail it back."

Lilah's heart sank. She understood what Nick was telling her. If you call, you'll ruin their trip. Her baby sister had been through so much pain before she'd met Chase Reynolds and his young son. She was married now and happy again. She deserved every carefree moment she could grab with her family.

Lilah stared at Sara, who stared back. Nick's wry smile mocked them both. "Well, I'll leave you two to sort out the sleeping arrangements." He turned toward Sara, who eyed him ferociously. She hated to be made fun of and Nick always managed to do it without saying a word.

Plopping her fisted hands on hips as slender as a teen's, she groused, "Why the devil are you here, Nick?"

"To tell you that Kurt Karpoun and Sam Henning are fighting again over that strip of land between their places. I saw Kurt sitting on his roof with a rifle full of buckshot."

Sara swore. "Well, why didn't you say so as soon as you came in?" Marching to the door, she grabbed her hat off a rack and jammed it on her head. Drawn by their voices, Bree meandered toward Lilah.

"Are we gonna eat or not?" she demanded, sparing only a single dismissive glance in Sara's direction and no acknowledgement at all for Nick. "You said we'd eat when we got here. Or did you mean when we got to a real town, with, like, an actual mall?"

Lip curled in disgust, Sara dug into her pants pocket. "Polite little thing, isn't she?" Withdrawing a set of keys, she tossed them to Lilah. "There's food at my place. You can take your old room and put Miss Teenage America in Nettie's."

"I'm not a teenager yet," Bree said.

"Did I sound like accuracy was my point?"

Bree didn't know what to make of that, so she resorted to the classic eye roll.

Lilah thought of the balance in her checking account and decided she couldn't afford to look a gift horse in the mouth, even if the horse did know how to say "I told you so" in five languages.

"Thanks very much, Sara." Making a bigger effort, she asked, "Are you going to be home for dinner?"

"Doesn't look like it." She waved a hand. "Just help yourselves to whatever. See you later." Swinging open the door, she headed into the evening sun.

"Suppose I'd better follow her," Nick said, but without much urgency. "When she's in a bad mood, your sister's apt to light more fires than she puts out."

"And yet you're still hanging around," Lilah said, curious and feeling an affection for Nick, who had been their next-door neighbor and adopted big brother for years. Sara found Nick utterly infuriating, and vice versa.

He shrugged an eyebrow noncommittally. "It's a small town. I feel better when I know where the ticking bomb is." Smiling, he tipped his head. "We'll grab a coffee soon."

"That'd be nice."

Nick followed Sara outside and Bree moved a few steps closer to Lilah. "Who was he, an old boyfriend or something?" True to the perspective of youth, she emphasized "old." Lilah could have pointed out that she was only twenty-nine, but since she felt ancient these days, she buried her ego.

"Come on," she said, "we'll go to Sara's, and I'll feed you so you won't have to complain to the child welfare people."

Chapter Three

A quick tour of Sara's kitchen revealed that peanut butter cups, nacho cheese tortilla chips, two jars of bean dip and several cereal boxes—all offering a toy inside— were her idea of "food."

"That's not dinner!" Bree protested, echoing Lilah's sentiments exactly, so they got back in the car and headed to the only restaurant in town.

Ernie's Diner was dotted with locals when they entered at half past five. Lilah had changed clothes and repaired her makeup quite deliberately. She was now thoroughly overdressed as she led her charge to a booth all the way in the back of the restaurant.

After scanning the pink plastic menu, she decided on

a dinner salad for a dollar ninety-five, because before they'd left the house she'd tallied her checkbook again, hoping she'd added it up incorrectly the first four times. They weren't broke—yet—but she needed a job and she needed it fast.

"I have to go to the restroom. Will you order for me? Thousand Island on the side," she told Bree as she scooted off the cracked and taped leather of the aged booth.

Bree shrugged, her nose already buried in a tattered copy of *The Hobbit*.

With a deep breath for courage, Lilah picked her way to the front of the restaurant on high-heeled white-and-gold sandals, the hem of a filmy white sundress swirling around her knees. Shaking back her hair, which she'd brushed and left loose, she reached into her large straw bag for the gift she'd brought Ernie, the owner of the diner—a signed and framed headshot of George Clooney. She'd been supplying Ernie with autographed studio photos for years. He'd hung them all around the restaurant.

The pictures were easy enough to acquire; Lilah simply wrote a letter requesting an autographed eight-by-ten—like any other fan. To Ernie and his regular customers, however, the Hollywood memorabilia was proof that Lilah had hit the big time. They believed she knew all the stars whose photos she acquired. Lilah of course had never disabused them of the idea. Now she hoped to make Ernie's unmerited awe work in her favor.

In addition to the money left in her account, there remained a couple thousand dollars in a savings account Grace had left for Bree. Lilah was determined not to touch that money, no matter what. Bree needed to know there was something from her mother. Grace had been so worried. Lilah had performed her best acting job to date when she'd tried to assure her friend that their finances were fine. In fact, she'd lost her waitressing job for taking too much time off when Grace was ill. Lying to a dying woman—Lilah wasn't sure whether she'd committed her first act of mercy or sunk to a new low. The devoted mother had died assuming there was more.

For years Lilah had lied about her acting credits, simply by claiming that she had some good ones. She hoped that if she told Ernie she wanted a temporary waitress position so she could "research a role for the theater," he might hire her, and she wouldn't have to admit she was almost thirty, that her bank account ran on fumes and that by most standards, especially her own, she was a big fat flop.

Reaching the cash register, Lilah glanced around the restaurant, spotting Mrs. Kay, the organist at Kalamoose First Baptist Church, along with several diners who were strangers to her, and she saw a waitress she didn't recognize…but no Ernie.

The waitress, a ringer for a young Natalie Wood, approached the register. Lilah wondered vaguely if Ernie had hired the girl knowing her looks would be good for business. Fresh and glowing with no sign yet of age or disillusionment. Lilah remembered when people had hired her based on youth and beauty alone.

Feeling a lifetime older than the flawless child before her, she fought to dredge up the smile that had made her Miss Kalamoose Creamery 1990-1992 and asked to see Ernie.

The girl stared at her blankly. "Ernie?" Wrinkling her pert nose, she cocked her head. "Um, a guy named Elmer comes in around five most nights for the chicken-fried steak. Do you mean him?"

Gorgeous, Lilah amended her first impression, *but thick as a post.* "Nooo, I mean Ernie the *owner,*" she clarified, aiming her thumb over her shoulder. "The one whose name is on the sign out front."

For a long moment, the girl gazed at Lilah with a little furrow between her dark eyebrows. "I didn't know there was a real Ernie. I thought it was just a name. You know, like Burger King."

"You mean, like Carl's Junior?"

"Is he real, too?"

"I think so. Anyway, I know Ernie is real, so is he around? In the back, perhaps?"

Suddenly the furrow cleared. "Oh, yeah, the owner's in back." A bell dinged in the kitchen. "That's my order. I've gotta go. Back in a sec." She disappeared before Lilah could remind her to send Ernie out.

Sighing, Lilah turned and walked to the wall of publicity photos Ernie had hung by the front door. Gazing idly at the pictures while she waited, she leaned forward suddenly as she recognized the first picture she'd ever sent home. This one wasn't a headshot; it was a reprint of a photo taken on the set of the only movie she'd ever done: *Attack Girls From Planet Venus*. The snapshot showed her and several other wanna-be starlets in scanty, strategically ripped silver attire. Lilah stood on the far right. Beneath her likeness she had written *To Ernie, I'll always love your milk shakes best. XOXO, Lilah*. Then she'd drawn a star instead of her last name.

Lilah shook her head. She didn't draw stars anymore. No one ever asked for her autograph, anyway.

"I didn't see that movie. The locals tell me it's a classic."

The deep voice, low and slow and sardonic, made Lilah's heart jump to her throat. She whirled around to find Gus standing mere inches behind her. Looming several inches taller and wider than she, he gazed over her head at the photograph then down again at her and raised an eyebrow with perfect irony.

"Was there a sequel?"

His presence seemed to surround Lilah, to press in on her, though there was a good foot and a half of air between them.

She stood dry-mouthed and thick-tongued as Gus's prairie-winter eyes lowered slowly from the photo to her face. Not sure what to expect from him, she felt a thin, sharp stab of anxiety as their gazes met and held. In all the years she'd known him, she had never stood this close without feeling the almost electric energy that pulsed between them. It had been there ever since they'd both hit puberty. Today was no different.

When she'd pictured him over the years—and she'd be lying through her teeth to claim that she hadn't—she had sometimes imagined him still in love with her and unable to mask the longing and youthful hunger that smoldered in his gaze. Once upon a time being with Gus had made her feel more special than she'd felt anyplace else.

Then there were the times in the past few years when Lilah could not picture Gus except as he'd looked the last time she saw him—with his eyes spitting sparks of fury and bitterness that had burned her soul.

Today if his eyes were a true indication of his feelings, he was long past the fury and resentment. Past the adolescent lust, too. In front of her was a man whose emotions were under his own control, and he looked at her with decided neutrality.

"The movie," he murmured, nudging her focus. "Was there ever a sequel?"

"I hope not."

He laughed at that. Easily. It was a sound she had not heard often from him. Even in their happiest moments and even though they'd almost always been alone together, away from the townspeople he'd mistrusted, Gus had rarely laughed. She remembered wanting him to, wanting to be the one to elicit a guffaw or two. Though she'd rarely been successful, she had challenged his control in other ways....

"So, what brings you back to town, Lilah?" The rich baritone, much deeper than she recalled, wrapped around her name. "Taking a break from the bright lights and big city?"

She looked for sarcasm and found none, but felt embarrassed nonetheless. Gus had no way of knowing that the brightest light she'd worked under in years was the plate warmer at Jerry's Deli. "My family is here," she said, striving for a matter-of-fact inflection, but to her own ears she sounded defensive. "I've been back many times over the years. Have you?"

She already knew the answer to that question, of course. She'd looked for him, listened for some clue to his whereabouts on most of those early visits home. But the only person in town who had ever kept tabs on Gus had been Uncle Harm, and he'd never spoken of Gus again after the time he'd called California to tell Lilah that Gus had been sentenced to one year in prison.

"My family left the area years ago," Gus told her dispassionately. "I had no reason to come back until recently."

No reason. Meaning *she* had not been a good enough reason. Lilah had always wondered if he'd ever looked her up.

Guess now I have an answer. Unwillingly, she felt hurt. As badly as they'd ended, she'd Googled him on the Internet lots of times, always warning herself to do nothing if his name came up, but never quite certain how she would react.

"Why *are* you back in town?" she asked. In high

school, nine-tenths of their conversations had centered not on *if* but rather on *when* they planned to make their permanent escapes.

"I'm building my home and business here."

"You're going to *stay...in Kalamoose?*" Surprise teemed with the ramifications this news posed, and Lilah felt dizzy.

God really does have a sense of humor.

With her mind a jumble of *oh, no's* and *what now's,* Lilah felt an almost desperate desire to rush back to the table, tell Bree they were going to dine on Sara's Cap'n Crunch after all and get the heck out of here so she could think.

Gus did weird things to her common sense—like obliterate it, entirely. It didn't matter how wrong they were for each other, how overcomplicated and flat-out painful her life had become because she hadn't been able to keep her adolescent hands off him; he was like a drug—she was forever yearning for him, even when her mind should have been on something, or perhaps somebody, else.

She forced herself to admit, albeit silently, that for the past twelve years she had unconsciously pasted Gus's countenance over the face of every man to whom she'd tried to get close. She'd had other lovers, two with whom she'd honestly tried to make a relationship work. But she had never been able to give herself wholly, and she had not understood why...until the night she'd realized that the arms she'd felt holding her, the hands she'd imagined caressing her, belonged to Gus and not to the man she was actually with. Bone-deep loneliness had dogged her for years; in that moment she'd understood why—and why the embrace of a lover had been no defense against it.

The best, the absolute wisest thing Lilah could do for herself would be to stay out of Gus's sight line. She had a life—two lives now—to put in order. Nothing good would come of continued contact with a man whose very presence had always ruined her ability to think.

She'd made too many mistakes in her relationship with Gus to believe they could pick up where they'd left off, and standing so close to him now, thinking things she prayed her face would not reveal, Lilah felt a traitorous bloom of red creep up her neck. She was trying to think of a polite way to excuse herself, to buy a little time so she could regroup before she saw him again, when he surprised her once more.

"I'm planning a large party in September," he said smoothly. It was a comment so utterly uncharacteristic of him, Lilah wasn't sure she heard correctly. In high school, he had never gone to a party, much less thrown one.

Now he gazed down at the girl who used to *be* his party and said with detached ease, "If you're here in the fall, be sure to drop by and help us celebrate."

September. Two months away. Lilah was no longer certain she should plan to stay in Kalamoose two weeks much less two months. Between her eyebrows, her head began to throb.

Say something, a voice inside urged. With her tongue feeling too thick to fit her mouth, she forced herself to ask, "What will you be celebrating?"

A satisfied smile crawled leisurely across Gus's handsome face. He looked every inch the contented man and every inch a success—proof that America was still the land of self-made men and second chances—when he answered.

"My marriage."

Whomp. Satisfaction hit Gus like a sock to the solar plexus. Confirmation, validation…retaliation. You name it, he felt it. And it felt fine.

He'd waited twelve years to see Lilah Owens swallow a bite, just a bite, of the shock and pain she'd fed him. The fact that their relationship was over a decade old and that her choices then could be blamed on youth and immaturity didn't appease his anger. He was surprised the resentment still burned so brightly all these years later.

He'd had a counselor once—in prison—who had helped him work on the concepts of forgiveness and letting go. After his initial resistance to everything the man had to say, Gus had learned a few things. Unfortunately none of the lessons he'd taken with him managed to completely obliterate his resentment. Nonetheless, even *he* was surprised by the degree of gratification he felt when Lilah registered the news that he was going to be married.

First, shock sparked in the gray-green eyes. Then the arched golden eyebrows pinched as if the news disturbed her. Gus watched her and had to work hard to keep his own expression under control when jealousy streaked across her face, briefly but unmistakably. He hadn't known he could still affect her. God help him, but the knowledge was rewarding.

Still beautiful, Lilah was close to thirty. One of the single secretaries at his office in Chicago had celebrated her thirtieth birthday on a Friday and by Monday had begun reacting to every marriage announcement with near suicidal grief. Perhaps Lilah was the same.

He'd already noted her bare ring finger. Some women chose not to wear a wedding ring, but he doubted Lilah Owens would be one of them. He imagined she would wear a rock the size of Gibraltar. She had never been quiet, never blended in. That had been his goal in school: to be so unremarkable that no one would pay attention to the son of the least respectable family in town.

He'd once thought Lilah wanted to keep their relationship a secret because, like him, she'd thought it was a special thing, too important to expose to the judgments of a bigoted town. He'd trusted her, one hundred percent.

Unbidden came the memory of the nights he'd lain awake in the barn where he'd often slept as a kid, gazing through the dark at the bare rafters and planning how to buy Lilah an engagement ring. He'd spent hours wondering if a ruby might be less expensive than a diamond, wondering how to get the money and where to buy a gem. In retrospect, nothing more than a fantasy for a kid who didn't have a mattress to sleep on.

He could buy Lilah a hundred rings now, he thought as he stared at her, a blood-red, passionate ruby or a diamond whose white brilliance set it for ever apart from the pale. But now it didn't matter, not for her.

Schooling his features to reflect dispassion, he said, "What can I do for you, Lilah?"

"C-congratulations."

They spoke over each other then hesitated and did it again.

"Thank you," he said.

"What?" she asked.

"Nikki said you asked to speak to me," Gus said. "What about?"

Lilah looked genuinely confused. "Nikki?" She glanced to the dining room. "The waitress?" Shaking her head, she corrected, "I asked to speak with Ernie."

Gus scratched his temple and tried to appreciate the irony. So Lilah *hadn't* sought him out? And here he'd been enjoying the indecency of power.

"Nikki said you wanted to speak to the owner," he told her, putting two and two together for both of them. "She obviously thought you meant me. I bought the diner from Ernie a month ago." This time he tried to keep the pride and challenge out of his voice. It finally began to sink in that standing here, hoping to inspire envy with news of his new home and wife-to-be was not only immature, it was hardly fair to his fiancée.

"If you need to speak with Ernie," he said with a customer-service politeness he had seldom exercised, "I'm sure we can help with that."

Lilah felt her heart lurch, indecisive and arrhythmic. She wasn't sure her exhausted body could take any more surprises than she'd already had today. "This is your business? The diner? I thought the gas station—"

"Also mine."

She tried to smile, to look as if she were pleased, but her face felt stiff, as if she'd overdosed on BOTOX. She knew she *should* be happy for Gus; he had apparently succeeded in the areas of life she had somehow managed to bungle—career and romance. But every new nugget of information he revealed complicated her situation more and more. Rather than being happy, she felt more scared, more lost, more alone by the second.

"Do you have Ernie's home number?" Gus broke into her thoughts. "I'm sure he'd enjoy hearing from you," Gus said with all the personalization of a cruise director pairing people up for a square-dance class. "Or if you prefer, he comes in for breakfast most mornings. You could catch him then."

And risk seeing Gus again before she had a chance to think...or take a large valium? "That's not necessary. Thanks, anyway. I only stopped in to...to give him this." She thrust the wrapped publicity photo out to Gus. "It's more for the diner. It's another photo. You're welcome to it." She made a face. "Or if you're going to change the decor, perhaps you could pass it to Ernie next time you see him."

She began to back up toward the booth where she'd left Bree. So much for a job at the only restaurant in town. Lilah decided swiftly and definitively that she'd made a mistake—another one—by coming home. Bree didn't like it here, anyway…not that Bree was going to like any place without Grace.

"I've got to get back to my—" She hitched a thumb over her shoulder, "To…Bree."

Instantly, Gus's eyes shifted to the booth where Bree sat with her head still bent over her book. Lilah cursed herself for calling attention to the girl. Pointing her out would only invite questions and more conversation.

"Well, good to see you again, Gus," she said, trying hard to convey the dispassion he seemed able to portray quite easily. "Best of luck with everything."

To underscore her nonchalance, she managed a classic hair flip when she turned away. The one she'd perfected in high school. The flip that said *I'm confident, I'm free, nothin's botherin' me.* To reinforce the image, she made herself swing around one last time, flashing a smile she didn't feel. "Is the chicken-fried steak still the best in North Dakota?"

Gus nodded. "Everything's the same."

Not hardly, Lilah thought, but she nodded, turned and

walked back to the booth, where she intended to encourage Sabrina to eat without chewing so they could get the hell out of here.

Chapter Four

"Forty-one, forty-two, forty-three, forty-four…"

Lilah pushed coins across the scarred butcher-block table in Sara's kitchen. She counted all the way to forty-eight dollars, looked at the money sitting in front of her and slumped until her cheek rested on the old pine.

The heavy thump of her heart and steady march of black hands across a cow-shaped kitchen clock provided the only background music to the impending disaster that had become her life.

It was ten minutes to 12:00 a.m. Between sips of hot cocoa laced with Irish Crème Liqueur, Lilah had counted and recounted every crumpled dollar bill and every sticky piece of change she'd scrounged from the bottom of her purse. She'd have to make another withdrawal from her checking account soon.

Groaning, she pounded a fist on the table—just once, because she was exhausted.

When Grace was sick, Lilah had asked her coworkers to sub for her so many times that eventually the manager had hired someone else. Then there had been the enticing dinners she had bought from the gourmet market to tempt Grace to eat, and the aromatherapy candles and food supplements and Chinese herbal remedies and organic potions and all the other ways Lilah had fought to keep Grace alive, to pretend they actually had some power in an ultimately powerless position.

Lilah's bank account had dwindled, and she hadn't been able to catch up. Still, she would learn how to cook cardboard boxes before she'd spend what was left of Grace's savings. She'd counted on getting a job at Ernie's. Jobs were not plentiful in rural North Dakota.

"I'm screwed. I'm just screwed," she said, shaking her head as she pushed away from the kitchen table.

She'd gone to bed around nine—before, thank goodness, Sara had come home from her final patrol of the night. Lilah simply hadn't wanted to talk to anyone, not until she'd had at least a little rest and could make some sense of her situation. Unfortunately, she hadn't slept a wink, and her situation wasn't looking any more sensible at 12:00 a.m. than it had when she'd gotten home from the diner.

Heaving her exhausted body out of the chair, she

shuffled to the pantry, wondering if Sara had any Scooter Pies. May as well ditch the diet she'd been on for the past twelve years. Her career was dead, her romantic life was a non-issue, and when everyone discovered the lie she had been living with for more than a decade, it was possible that no one, not even her own sisters, would want to speak to her.

Settling for a handful of Cap'n Crunch with Crunch Berries, she ate over the sink, listening to her teeth grind the cereal and watching pink Crunch Berry crumbs dapple the scratched porcelain basin. When she finished, she stared through the window at the high half moon. She'd come home for comfort.

She'd come home hoping that her sisters—and she figured Nettie was her best bet—would see that taking care of Bree was wearing her nerves down to nubs. *Look at you,* her baby sister would say, *you're exhausted. This is too much for someone who is not used to children. Let me help.*

The thought that had brought transient relief on the drive to North Dakota now turned the cereal sour in her stomach.

Standing still, Lilah covered her face with her hands. She wasn't the one who had died, wasn't the one who had slipped unwillingly away from a daughter she'd raised and nurtured and needed like a star needs the night to shine. Yet here she was, filled with worry, feeling sorry for herself and wanting someone to rescue her.

When she saw Gus at the restaurant and heard that

he was building a home and a business in Kalamoose, there had been a part of her that thought—for a split second—that perhaps fate had decided they were not through after all. Perhaps that angry boy who had been all wrong for her at seventeen, but whom she had never been able to forget, was going to be her knight in shining armor now that they were both adults.

Maybe, she'd thought before he'd mentioned a fiancée, *everything that's happened was supposed to bring us together again.*

Turning on the faucet, Lilah splashed her face with cold water. "You have become a poor excuse for a woman with a brain," she muttered.

Twisting the squeaky knob again and drying her hands on the dishtowel Sara left draped over the faucet, Lilah braced her arms against the sink and hung her head. Gus Hoffman had spent the past twelve years creating a life that would give him contentment while she had morphed from a girl who had planned to conquer the world into a woman who wished someone would rescue her.

Pathetic.

All night she'd been fighting the memory of his expression as he told her he was getting married. He'd looked proud, but more importantly, satisfied. In the past, albeit the distant past, he had looked that way only when he was with her.

Hot and restless, she pulled at the neck of her tank top then reached over the sink to open the window and let in some air. Grunting, she pushed ineffectively at the frame until she realized that Sara had installed some funky new lock.

Dang Sara and her security measures. This is Kala-moose, not freaking L.A.

The thought had barely formed in her brain when she saw a shadow through the window. The shadow of a person standing in their yard.

At 12:00 a.m.

Lilah's first impulse was to yell for her sister, but she didn't want to alarm Bree, and she felt a sudden surge of adrenaline that told her to fight, not flee. She lived in Los Angeles, for crying out loud; she'd had her car broken into three times. She could deal with one small-town Peeping Tom.

Racing barefoot to the kitchen door, she grabbed the battered baseball bat that had stood sentinel for years— ever since Sara had placed it there to threaten the raccoons that routinely made a mess of their garbage cans.

Dousing the lights, Lilah peeked through the curtain covering the kitchen door window. The helpful moon bathed the person in the yard in an eerie glow, outlining the silhouette of a rather large man. Clearly, he'd seen her through the window. Now that she'd turned off the lights, he appeared to be waiting, though for what she had no idea. He stood stock-still, neither approaching the house nor turning to leave before he was caught.

The arrogance, Lilah thought and then immediately was struck by a rush of déjà vu so strong she felt transported to another time. Another time…but the very same place.

Unlatching Sara's collection of dead bolts, she turned the knob on the kitchen door and stepped outside. Cool air bathed her bare legs and whispered softly around her shoulders and arms. Still clutching the bat, she shivered.

I know this moment. She'd lived it thirteen summers ago, though without the baseball bat that time. Just sixteen, awake with the thrill of secret love, she had flown outside under the light of this very moon to her lover's arms. She recognized him now, thought he'd thrown no stones at her window and showed no intention of running eagerly across the lawn to meet her halfway.

Tonight Gus merely watched her as she descended the porch steps and walked toward him slowly, feeling vaguely as if she'd fallen asleep at the table and was dreaming this whole thing.

She walked until she saw his face clearly, stopping a few feet away.

His eyes roamed down her body, taking in the loose, mussed hair, sleeveless nightshirt, bare legs. Then his gaze wandered up again while hers traveled over a muscular frame dressed in a T-shirt and jeans. They studied each other unabashedly, like naked lovers viewing their partners for the first time.

She felt the old heady recklessness that had pumped her full of life every time Gus met her at night—despite rules, despite curfews, despite being too young to deal with any consequences. The struggle to suppress the feeling seemed, rather, to inflame them more. For a moment, she wanted to forget everything, every excellent reason for keeping her distance from him now, and simply fall into a wordless kiss.

The idea that she might be willing to ignore the fact that he had a fiancée repulsed her. She had been a lot of things—selfish, dishonest, shallow at times—but she had never yet been an adulteress.

"You're trespassing," she informed Gus in a voice roughened by suppressed emotion.

He glanced to the makeshift weapon in her hand. "You've got a bat and a sister who's the sheriff—you want me gone, do something about it."

"What are you doing here?"

A long moment passed before Gus answered. She wasn't sure he was going to respond at all, but then he smiled, and in that second he looked like the old Gus—cocky, irreverent, *bad*.

"The same thing all ex-cons do, Lilah," he said in a silky voice intended to travel no farther than her ears. He took three lazy steps toward her, and the glint in his eyes was positively sinful. "I'm returning to the scene of my crime."

"What crime would that be?" Lilah said, her heart beating against her chest as she strove to appear calmer than she felt. "I thought your crime was drag racing along Main Street."

"You mean when I crashed my car into Old Man Hertzog's grocery?" Gus leaned indolently against the doorframe. He crossed his arms, as relaxed as if they chatted about old times every night around midnight. "Not the crime to which I refer," he said, a corner of his mouth hooking into a half smile. "I'm talking about the crime that happened a couple years earlier than that. The crime of falling for the sheriff's niece."

"It's almost midnight," she protested, mindful of Sara and Bree asleep—she hoped—upstairs. "You shouldn't be here."

"I was never supposed to be here. Didn't bother you before."

"Seems like stating the obvious to say we've both changed since then." She tugged at the hem of her tank top, ineffectively trying to make it stretch past the short tap pants she slept in during the summer. "What do you want?"

In lieu of answering, he poked his head over hers and looked around the kitchen. "Invite me in, Lilah. Do you know I've never seen the inside of this house before?"

"I don't think that's a good idea."

"Why? Afraid I won't like the decor?"

"I don't think it's a good idea for you to come in this late," she clarified tightly. "My sister…"

The gray eyes she used to get lost in so easily narrowed and turned cold. "Never liked me," he finished for her. The relaxed smile around his lips tensed—not much, but enough for her to notice. "I have my own shower at home now, and my clothes are almost always clean. I don't think I'll offend anyone."

"That's not what I mean, and you know it!" Her face

felt hot, but the bare wood of Sara's kitchen floor sent a chill through her bones.

There was no point in contending that she'd never been offended by him, not by his clothes or his family or by any of the other things that had shamed him in his youth. There was no point, because it wasn't true.

The first time she'd seen Gus, she'd been curious and a little scared. At the age of ten, she'd moved with her sisters from Seattle, Washington, to Kalamoose, North Dakota. The girls' parents had died in a plane crash on their way home from a second honeymoon. Up to that time, the Owens sisters had lived a sheltered, gentle life. Raised by parents who had loved each other and adored their children, Lilah and her sisters had had no reason to expect anything but the joy to which they were accustomed. Lilah wasn't sure about Nettie or Sara, but the accident that took her parents' lives had changed something in her, something deep and crucial.

She wasn't sure she could articulate the change even now, as an adult; she certainly hadn't been able to do it as a child. All she knew was that her parents had left full of happiness, that they'd expected the best from life and had suffered the worst; they'd been torn from their kids, and at some point before they'd died there must have been a moment, a cruel and heartaching moment, when together they'd known, they'd never see their girls again.

The moment Lilah had realized her parents were lost to her forever was the moment she'd stopped feeling loved and had started to feel abandoned. Not by her parents, but by the universe. In some ways, that was worse.

She'd arrived in North Dakota shaky, confused and afraid for some reason to tell anyone what she was feeling. At that time she had wanted nothing more than to fit in, to be loved not only by Uncle Harm, who had his hands more than full with three preteen girls dropped on his doorstep, but to be loved and admired and accepted by everyone—students, teachers, the town. She'd had the idea that if she was really special, truly loved, then God would think she was valuable, and He wouldn't let anything bad happen again. It was a child's reasoning, but she'd taken it right into adulthood.

She'd begun her acting career on the first day she'd attended her new school. Masking her anxiety with smiles, she'd attempted to fill the large woundlike hole inside her with friends who would follow her anywhere. By her twelfth birthday, she'd been firmly established as the most popular girl in seventh grade, and she'd all but forgotten the hollow fear inside. She'd already been crowned Junior Chokecherry Princess; the whole town knew her. Then her Uncle Harm had decided it was time to add a few good deeds to her list of accomplishments. That was how she'd gotten to know Gus, utterly against her own will....

"But I'm invited to Cathie Lyn's house for lunch today. All the girls will be there!"

Lilah stared pleadingly at her uncle from across the

breakfast table. *All the girls* were Lilah's three best friends from middle school, and today was the day they were going to figure out how to get four ninth-grade boys to ask them to the fall barn dance, even though Lilah and her friends were only in seventh grade.

Uncle Harm scraped his chair back and rose to get another cup of coffee. "You can catch up with your friends later, honey. This won't take all day." His voice was the soothing blend of firmness and courtesy that made him a respected sheriff. "First, I want you to pick the box of clothes up from the church and bring it to my office." He repeated his original request, adding, "When Gus gets there, you can help him sort out what he wants and take the rest back to the church."

"Why can't he go to the church?"

"It'll feel less like charity if we do it this way."

Harm's quiet dignity ought to have persuaded his niece, even made her feel good about helping, but Lilah could think only that she didn't want to spend her Saturday rummaging through old clothes that reeked of mothballs.

She especially didn't want to miss such an important meeting to spend time with Gus Hoffman. She would never live it down, if she even survived it.

"I can't *believe* you'd let your own niece be alone with him," she accused. "He's going to grow up to be a thief, or maybe a serial killer. I'll probably be his first victim. Everyone knows his family has bad blood."

She felt the change in Uncle Harm's demeanor before she looked up and saw it.

Silence, heavy and admonishing, hung in the room like fog. Sara stopped chewing, and their younger sister, Nettie, who'd been minding her own business, now glanced at Lilah with equal parts surprise and concern.

"Well, it *is* what everybody says," Lilah mumbled, picking up her fork to poke holes in her pancake.

Harm took a sip of coffee, set the mug on the counter and crossed his arms. His gaze never left her. "I hope you set them straight." When Lilah didn't answer, Harm picked up a dishtowel—and still managed to look like God.

He turned toward the sink and wiped a coffee mug that had been drying from earlier that morning. "Some folks don't look beyond a person's appearance or their past," he stated calmly. "That says more about the person doing the looking than it does about the one being looked at."

"Sure does." Sara nodded around another pork link.

The half pancake Lilah had eaten grew heavy in her stomach. At fourteen, Sara didn't even own a lipstick; of course she hoped no one judged her by appearances. Lilah knew better.

Setting down her fork, she fingered one of the long blond curls she'd painstakingly wound around hot rollers this morning. She might be only twelve, but she was already aware that she could use her looks to make people forget that she wasn't as smart as Sara or as sweet as Nettie.

Gus Hoffman never tried to make anyone like him, which was probably why nobody did. It wasn't her fault that he wore ratty clothes; the church ladies were always giving decent things away. She and her sisters had worn plenty of their hand-me-downs. And it wasn't her fault that he never cut his hair, or that he attended school mostly when he felt like it. Adults were always going on and on about choices; why should she suffer for Gus Hoffman's?

Last year he'd been in school only a few weeks before he'd punched Billy Grant in the nose, because Billy had called him a half-breed. Billy's nose had bled all the way through third period English. How come Uncle Harm didn't think about that?

"I don't see why he needs clothes, anyway," she grumbled, eliciting a worried, under-the-table pinch from Nettie. "He hardly ever comes to town, and when he does, he's got his head in a garbage can. He's going to make the clothes stink."

She knew she'd gone too far, but she couldn't stop herself. She didn't know why, but whenever she saw Gus pawing through garbage like an animal, something inside her got prickly hot and angry. People stared at him, and except for the time he'd socked Billy, he didn't react. Lilah kind of thought she should be angry with the people who mocked him, but instead she found her resentment directed toward Gus. Why couldn't he try to fit in?

Instead of reprimanding her, Uncle Harm narrowed his eyes—like he was thinking, not like he was angry—and nodded slowly. "Gus searches through the garbage because he collects bottles and cans and returns them to the store for money." He let that sink in a minute then added, "It's true he hasn't been to school much. I'm glad you see that as a troubling thing, Lilah. It's been troubling me, too. I visited your principal, and she agrees with us, so Gus is going to attend school regularly starting next week."

Harm picked up the griddle he'd washed earlier and wiped it methodically. "He's been working hard to catch up in school. When he gets there, I want him to feel as comfortable as possible. Go through the clothes and help him pick what the other boys are wearing these days. The ladies at church are generous, but their taste isn't always up to the times." Harm turned his head and smiled. "And he'll need some help getting reacquainted with the kids and making a fresh start."

Oh, no...

"I told Mrs. Wilhelm I was sure you'd volunteer for that job."

Oh, no, no, no!

Sara snorted orange juice through her nose.

Nettie, who up to now had remained silent, interjected sweetly, "He'll like that. Lilah knows everyone!"

Lilah felt dizzy. She had only one more year of middle school. High school was just around the corner. There were things you could and could not do if you wanted people to like you. Forcing your friends to eat lunch with Gus Hoffman was one of the things you could not do. She'd be an outcast.

The thought of being lonely again…not sought after by the other kids, not special…

Lilah began to feel some of the nauseating dread she'd had when she'd first arrived in Kalamoose. Dropping her fork onto her plate, she pushed the pancakes away before she got sick all over the table.

As the nausea rose, however, so did anger—furious, heart-pounding rage at Gus Hoffman, who was about to ruin her life and wouldn't even be grateful when she helped him….

Standing in the doorway to Sara's home, Gus was, apparently, still confused by the concept of fitting in. Lilah looked at him and decided that he hadn't changed that much, really, since his wayward boyhood.

It was just around midnight, hardly an appropriate time to pay a social call to the home of a single woman in a small town, but he was here nonetheless, in a pair of Tommy Hilfiger jeans and shirt that showed he had no trouble choosing his own stylish clothes these days.

Lilah felt herself staring at the V neck of his shirt and the dark caramel skin that reflected the Lakota half of his ancestry. She remembered that indentation between his collarbones. She'd first noticed it the year she and Gus had turned fifteen, first kissed it when they were sixteen.

Flooding with heat, she jerked her gaze to his face. "Sara is asleep. That's what I was about to say. You shouldn't be here. It isn't seemly."

Humor edged his mouth. "Really. It's not seemly?"

He was laughing at her. *Seemly* would hardly describe their midnight encounters in high school.

Lilah bristled. "Does your fiancée approve of your paying midnight calls to the neighbors?"

The smile didn't exactly leave Gus's face, but it hardened, became something that didn't reach his eyes. "Karen is out of town."

Tilting her head so that her hair fell over one eye, Lilah smiled. It was a provocative look she'd practiced since tenth grade, one that almost always gave her a sense of power. "What she doesn't know won't hurt her?"

Gus looked her right in the eye.

"*I* won't hurt her. Karen isn't threatened by high school relationships that ended in high school."

Chapter Five

Score: Gus one, Lilah zero. The ulcer she was sure she was nursing started to burn. Glancing at a cupboard, she wondered if Sara had any Maalox. Unwelcome curiosity about Gus's intended bride invaded her thoughts. He and Lilah had been *kids* in love. Looking back, and looking beneath their facades, they'd both been lonely and hungry for connection. Could what they'd shared be called love with the light of adulthood shined on it? Now Gus was a grown-up *in love* with another grown-up, and Lilah couldn't help but wonder if he'd chosen someone calm, someone capable and steady and kind. Someone not…her.

"If you're going to be here long," he drawled with enviable offhandedness, "I'm sure you'll meet Karen."

Swell.

"She'll be moving here from Illinois in a few weeks. Right now she's in Florida, visiting her grandparents."

Karen had family. Lilah felt an utterly inappropriate surge of jealousy as she imagined Gus sitting around a table full of laughter at Thanksgiving.

She and Gus had never spent a holiday together. He'd always claimed to be unconcerned with the festivities other people thought were so special, and holidays hadn't felt natural to her, anyway, since her parents had died. Uncle Harm, a lifelong bachelor, hadn't had a clue about how to cook a turkey or decorate a tree. Their first few holidays together had been spent at other people's homes, borrowing other people's traditions. Once Nettie was old enough, she turned all her innate nurturing instincts toward recreating a sense of celebration in their own home, but by that time Thanksgiving and Christmas, especially, had seemed sad to Lilah.

The last few years, she'd told Nettie she was in a play and couldn't get away. In reality, she'd stayed in L.A. to work the evening shift at the restaurant on Thanksgiving and Christmas. Since Nettie's marriage, she felt like an interloper.

Apparently Gus had finally found what she had lost and never recovered, and what he had never had to begin with. She should be happy for him. Instead, an altogether disturbing envy curled through her veins like smoke. She didn't begrudge Gus his chance to experience family, but the jealousy she felt toward his fiancée,

Karen, for being the one to give him those things was altogether unsettling.

To cover her discomfort, she nodded and smiled with what she hoped looked like a lack of concern. "That's nice. Listen, thanks for stopping by, but it's late."

She tried to shut the door, but he put out a hand, easily blocking her effort.

"I brought you something, Lilah, and I came all this way to give it to you in private, so don't be rude."

"What do you want, Gus?"

He reached into the pocket of his trousers to withdraw a round, gold watch and chain and dangled it in front of her.

Lilah gasped. "Harm's pocket watch."

Reverently she reached out to touch the elegant timepiece, caught off guard by a swell of emotion that made her throat ache. She ran a shaky finger over the initials engraved on the cover. The pocket watch Harm had rarely been without was a huge part of her memory of him.

"Where did you get it? We looked everywhere for it after he died. We thought it had been stolen."

She looked up to catch Gus watching her, his jaw set, his eyes more flinty than they'd been yet, as if her show of emotion annoyed him. There was animosity in that gaze.

Lilah yanked her hand from the watch and covered her mouth. *Oh, no.*

Suspicion began its slick, insidious crawl through her blood. Had Gus taken the watch? In the end, he had hated her and been furious with Harm, too. Had his rage been strong enough to make him betray the one man who had helped him?

She didn't have to say a word for Gus to know what she was thinking.

His expression grew colder still. "Atta girl, Lilah. Expect the worst before you ask any questions." Bitterness tarnished his laugh. "I suppose I should have seen that coming."

"That's not fair!" Even when he'd hot-wired a car to drag race down Main Street and wound up crashing into Hertzog's Grocery—and her own uncle had been forced to arrest him—even then, her first impulse had been to deny any wrongdoing on Gus's part. "I never expected the worst of you, Gus. I was on your side—"

"In private." His gaze roamed deliberately over her body, lingering on her bare legs before traveling back to her face. "Yes, you were. I never had to worry about your loyalty when we were alone. That's something, I suppose."

He leaned forward, so close she could feel his breath on her face. Before she could defend against it, the memory of his kiss rushed in, making her dizzy and hot. Gus knew what she was thinking—she could tell—and he hovered a moment, letting her remember, letting her feel the difference between then and now.

"A boy can feel like a man when his girl runs to meet him in the dark." His whisper was slow, pointed, edgy. "A man knows that the only woman worth his time will

defend him in the light of day. You can't defend someone you won't even admit to dating."

He straightened a bit, just enough to watch her face.
"I was everything you wanted as long as it was just the
two of us. But I wasn't fit for company, was I, Lilah?"

He knew how to strike where it hurt the most.

"We *both* wanted to keep our relationship private,"
she reminded him, struggling against shame, because
she understood the not-so-fine line between *private* and
secret. What if she had insisted on bringing their relationship out in the open?

All her life she'd been a chameleon, trying to look,
sound and behave in certain ways to make herself ac-
ceptable. She hadn't been able to figure out a way to
make Gus fit the picture, so she'd lived two lives—
one in public and one with him. He had claimed he
wanted it that way, too, that he preferred to keep to
himself. She had believed him, because it had been
easier that way.

But what if she'd encouraged him to face his fears?
What if she'd openly dared the townspeople to accept
the boy she'd loved?

She looked at Gus now, at that proud jaw and the once
gentle gray eyes. How it must have stung to be kept forever on the outside of the community when the one you
loved might have had the power to bring you into the fold.

"It was a long time ago," she said, hoping that might
exonerate her, in his eyes and her own. Her voice reflected her raw feelings. "We were just kids."

"But we hurt each other like grown-ups."

She couldn't deny it.

After Harm had ordered her to help Gus choose clothes for school, Lilah had acted with only minimal grace. Gus hadn't been much more affable than she. While Lilah had rummaged through the boxes, he had flipped a flat rock in the air, pretending not to have any interest in what she was doing. Just for meanness, she'd stuck a couple of too-small shirts and pants in his take-home box, and he'd worn them to school as if he hadn't noticed a problem with them.

When the other kids had laughed, Gus, who'd already turned thirteen by that time, had pulled a cigarette butt from his pocket, lit it and shrugged toward Lilah. "Talk to my tailor."

For smoking on campus, he'd gotten himself kicked out of school before the final bell on the first day. When word had gotten back to Harm that Gus was wearing too-small clothes, Lilah had gotten grounded.

They'd mostly avoided each other after that, though occasionally over the next couple of years her friends would whisper and laugh and gossip about Gus when they saw him. And now and then when Lilah wasn't careful, she would stop by the sheriff's office intending to talk to her uncle or to track down one of her sisters, and she'd run into Gus, sweeping or mopping the cell floors for pocket money.

He'd lean on his broom, smile if she passed close enough and drawl so only she could hear, "Hey, tailor, gonna invite me to hang with your friends? I'll wear my best shirt." He'd laugh at her then continue with his work as if he hadn't noticed her at all.

Lilah would burn with anger and, for some reason she never could figure out, with shame for the rest of the day.

Then one afternoon, a week after her fourteenth birthday, she'd walked into the sheriff's office when no one else was there. Except Gus...

Lilah opened the heavy wood door to the jail and entered quietly, intending not to interrupt Harm if he was immersed in desk work. Shuffling through papers made him cranky, and she needed to talk to him when he was in the best mood possible to increase the odds that he would say yes to her request.

She'd turned fourteen on Saturday, and for her birthday she wanted to buy the lovely dress she'd seen in a department store in Minot and go all out in her campaign to win a spot on the junior homecoming court. She considered the dress to be an excellent investment. She'd already won two local teen beauty pageants, after all. Practically the whole town knew about that. Now that she'd decided she wanted to be an actress and would go to Hollywood one day, she needed exposure. Being on the homecoming court would provide good experience in handling future public appearances.

Unfortunately Harm planned to give her fifty dollars for her birthday, and the dress cost eighty. She needed to ask him for an advance on next month's allowance, and getting that money wasn't going to be easy, because Uncle Harm was trying to teach them all to budget and had been talking about "living within one's means."

Lilah held her breath. She wanted the dress more than she could say, but she didn't know how to explain why. She knew only that when she imagined wearing the silky pale blue sheath, she could picture the faces of people she knew, smiling at her, looking admiring and it made her feel safe.

Moving quietly, she stepped farther inside the outdated jail. As her eyes adjusted to the dim light, she realized that Harm was not at his desk. The two cells on the left side of the large room were both empty.

She released the breath she'd been holding, a huge thud of disappointment weighing down her limbs, but as she turned to leave, a sound came from the storeroom and she began mentally rehearsing the argument for her cash advance. When she reached the storeroom, however, the sight that greeted her drove thoughts of money and even of the perfect dress from her mind.

Gus Hoffman stood by the old refrigerator in the corner. Light from the open fridge door backlit his every move. While Lilah watched, he took two slices of American cheese from the package Uncle Harm kept at work, opened one slice, ate it and jammed the other in the pocket of a badly frayed blue-jean jacket. Then he pulled a slice of white bread from a plastic-wrapped loaf and rolled a piece into a ball that he could fit into his mouth all at once.

When the second slice of bread joined the cheese in his pocket, Lilah realized how Gus's jacket hung on his body. Most of the boys in school were thin, but she hadn't noticed until now that Gus was just plain skinny.

As he reached for a half gallon of milk and prepared to drink it from the carton, she remembered the time he'd told Mr. Hertzog that he and his family didn't need food badly enough to accept charity. She knew Uncle Harm would give Gus something to eat—as much as he wanted—if only Gus asked. Just as certainly, she knew Gus never would. In fact, if Uncle Harm offered him anything, he'd probably claim he'd just had a meal.

Her first thought was how different she was from Gus—she who, if she'd been starving, would have smiled prettily at an offer of food and pretended she was at a dinner party. But then, watching Gus's profile, noting the way he closed his eyes as he drank the milk and the way he lowered his head after, she recognized the secret loneliness of a fifteen-year-old boy who hated charity, but stood in front of someone else's refrigerator and stole food. And she understood that she and Gus weren't so very different at all.

Intending to leave without anyone knowing she'd been there, she backed away from the storeroom door. A faux bronze statue of Buffalo Bill Cody sat atop a wooden table near the door. Lilah's hip connected with one of the table's corners and tipped the statue, which made a solid thunk as it rolled onto the floor.

Gus's head whipped toward her. Though the plastic

jug was still in his hand, he quickly backhanded the evidence of milk from his mouth. Surprise, humiliation and thunderous fury chased each other across his face. The sharp rise and fall of his chest made him look, Lilah thought, like something wild—a cornered animal, or the boy who had grown up with wolves.

After a long frozen moment, he burst into action, shoving the open milk jug into the refrigerator and cannoning toward her, eyes on fire. Caught off guard, she barely had time to become frightened before he backed her up near the door and slammed his hands against the wall, on either side of her head.

"Are you going to tell your uncle?"

"Uncle Harm wouldn't care—"

Gus slapped the wall. "Are you going to tell him?"

Lilah was the tallest girl in her class, but Gus was taller still, and she understood that he was trying to use that advantage to intimidate her.

"I'm not afraid of you," she said quietly, feeling her body settle because she realized it was true.

"If you tell him—" Gus halted the threat abruptly. He had no follow-through, because he knew what she knew: he wasn't going to hurt her in any way. He was the one who was frightened.

Moving slowly, she pushed one of his arms down, giving herself an escape route. His fist clenched by his side. She let him stare at her a long time, let him see that she wasn't going to sneer or mock him or laugh at him.

Taking several steps toward the main office, she

turned to face him. "I'm not going to tell." She paused then added, "Anyone."

She wasn't going to gossip about him. Whether or not he believed her, she knew right down to her bones that she would never again gossip about Gus Hoffman.

His brows buckled over his eyes.

Lilah hesitated a moment, feeling that something else should happen, though she didn't know what. Suddenly she noticed his nose, the way his nostrils flared as a wild animal's would, as if he were using her scent to gauge whether she was friend or foe. And then she noticed his scent—fresh hay and wild clover—and she wondered if he worked in someone's field when he didn't work for Harm, or whether he slept outside. The latter image suited him best. It even filled Lilah with a strange yearning simply to watch him as he lay on his back staring at the night sky, outdoors and away from everyone else, secret yet free.

When Gus continued to stare at her silently, familiar hot suspicion in his eyes, she realized no one knew how to talk to him, not even Harm.

Glancing at the open refrigerator, she told him matter-of-factly, "You'd better put everything away." Turning, she walked to the doorway that connected the front and rear sections of the jail. Without another look in his direction, she added, "Don't forget to cap the milk. Uncle Harm never leaves anything uncapped."

When Lilah looked at Gus now, no longer skinny, his expression still full of power and fury, she knew that the scene in Harm's storeroom would always be one of her strongest memories of him, the point at which everything changed. Everything.

"I'd have given the watch to one of your sisters," he said now, his tone tight, his eyes still accusing and resentful, "but I figured they'd throw me in jail without asking questions."

His words sparked more sadness, but a healthy dose of Lilah's indignation, too. "My sisters were never rude or cruel to you, Gus." It was true; Nettie would have taken him a box of clothes in two shakes, had Uncle Harm asked her.

Gus merely shrugged.

Frustrated, she threw up her hands. "Did you *really* want me to tell everyone we were together? Would that have been better?"

"Not at first," he admitted. "I took enough crap from this town without having to deal with its reaction to my dating the homecoming queen. But two years into it, when we were about to graduate, anyway? I think we could have come out of the closet by then, don't you?"

"Why didn't you say something then? You weren't exactly shy. Why didn't you tell me how you felt?"

"I shouldn't have had to."

Lilah shook her head, curled her hands into fists and pressed them to her hips. "You've always been damned self-righteous, you know that? And stubborn! You never wanted to listen to me or to anyone else."

"So now we know why it didn't work out between us."

Tension made Lilah's scalp tighten.

"After all these years are you really still so unforgiving?" she asked, realizing she'd been holding her breath for more than a decade, hoping someday they'd meet again and he'd let her in.

"After all these years, I've learned there are lessons you shouldn't forget."

A whirlpool of emotion made Lilah queasy. She pulled her lower lip between her teeth. Dealing with him on this trip home was simply too much for her. Even if she wanted to talk, he wasn't ready to listen. And there were other people in the picture, now—his fiancée, for one. There was certainly no way to avoid the awareness of him, but she could avoid dealing with him while he was so angry. She'd stay away from the diner, buy her gas in Anamoose....

She jumped when he brushed her lower lip with his thumb—roughly. Amber brows drew together in a scowl. "Stop chewing. You'll lose half your lip that way."

It was what he'd always said to her when she nibbled on her lower lip in times of uncertainty. Back then, of course, the pad of his thumb had danced across her lips like a feather. His voice had teased. The simple and caring act had never failed to stir her or to lead to a kiss... that would lead to something else.

Today his tone was anything but teasing and caring, and yet when he touched her, her body responded as if she were seventeen again.

The heat spread up and down.

Don't be an idiot. The thought thrummed through her

brain even as her breath grew shallow and she searched his gaze for some softening, some sign that he remembered the love that had come before the hate.

One look from Gus, one clandestine gaze from across a street, had always made her feel cherished. It was a feeling she'd searched for in so many other ways. Would things have turned out better if she'd allowed Gus's love to be enough?

He must have wondered the same thing, years ago. Today as he held on to her chin, his gray eyes were stormy and severe, and suddenly she needed to know that something of that softer time remained. It was a need that unfortunately trumped sense and overruled dignity.

"Why are you here, Gus?" She heard the scratch in her voice.

"I already answered that."

"But I don't believe you."

Tension quivered between them. His fingers tightened on her chin. He tilted her face toward his, and she let him. When he lowered his head to growl near her lips, she breathed him in.

"It was always a mistake, wasn't it, Lilah? Always a dangerous combination, you and I."

She felt his whisper on her face…warm. Prickles of heat skittered across her skin, but his words made her heart ache.

"Don't say we were *always* a mistake, Gus. Don't say that."

Once she'd burrowed in his arms in the middle of the

night, inhaled the scent of his warm skin and whispered to him, *You smell perfect. You smell so safe.* He'd laughed at her, but held on tighter. How could that moment, which was still one of the best of her life, be a mistake?

Even now, the closeness of his chest, his face, the height and breadth and heat of him made her feel she belonged to this place, to this moment. She wanted to stay here even though lately she felt like running away, no matter where she was.

Gus must have known he was standing too close for a man who was engaged, but he didn't move away.

"Don't call it a mistake?" he asked in a husky rasp. "What would you call this, tonight?"

He grasped her chin and tilted her face up. His voice lowered to an intimate caress. "I could kiss you right now. Your eyes always told me when you wanted to be kissed. They're talking to me now, Lilah."

He moved closer. She swallowed, admitting the truth with a tiny, tiny nod that said she knew her heart and soul, if not her mind and body, were still his.

She couldn't pull away, couldn't order him to stay back even though guilt and anxiety coursed through her.

If she tilted her face just a fraction more, her mouth would be his to claim....

"Don't worry, Lilah. I'm not going to kiss you. I gave up playing Russian roulette over you the day I walked into prison."

Chapter Six

Gus heard his own words, watched the scene as if he were standing outside himself, looking at someone else, and thought, *Poor dumb bastard, lying through his teeth*. His body nearly shook with desire. He was even starting to sweat.

Self-disgust ripped at him, pulling the lid off his anger. Releasing Lilah's chin, he reached for one of her hands and pressed the smooth gold of Harm's pocket watch into her palm.

"I thought Nettie might want this. I heard she has a son." He let go of her completely then and stepped back. "I never bore any ill will against your sisters, Lilah. And I don't hold a grudge against Harm. It was you who made me angrier than I ever knew I could be. But sitting in a jail with nothing much to do tends to clear your mind after a while. I realized I was angry at a mirage. What you offered only looked like love. People in love are loyal. They sacrifice. You never knew how to put anyone else first."

He watched Lilah's flushed face grow pale, far paler than its customary ivory. This should have been his crowning moment. A period on the end of a long, long sentence. But the reality put a steely taste in his mouth.

The green cat eyes he'd forced himself to remember as artful and deceiving now filled with pain, sharp and genuine. He tried to recall whether he'd ever seen that expression in her eyes before, but all he remembered was the golden girl of middle school and senior high. The girl who had seemed too bright and clean and special for him to touch. He remembered the laughter that sounded like bells, the ribbons of long blond hair flipping in the wind, a smile that lit an entire street.

God, how he'd wanted her, needed her, back then. She'd been the answer to patching together his heart, and it had already been torn so many times that until Lilah, he hadn't known it could come together again. When she'd loved him, he'd felt almost whole.

When she'd stopped loving him, another piece of his heart had ripped away, this wound jagged and raw and impossible to suture. Logic hadn't helped. Neither had time. Eventually he'd gone on, allowing the tear to stay as a reminder that no one should have as much power over another human as he'd given Lilah. But in that first moment of her betrayal—when he'd realized she didn't want him forever, as he'd wanted her—he'd felt so full of misery he'd have just as soon died. And he'd been so angry, he'd wanted to kill.

He looked at her now, as hurt by his cutting estimation of her actions as he'd hoped she would be. He waited for the anticipated relief. Waited for the recognition that he was finally done, finally free.

What he got instead was a flood of memories that managed to wash out the present, leaving him exposed and aching and remembering too clearly what it had been like to be eighteen and still in love....

Gus walked along the row of lockers at Kalamoose High, face set, gaze focused inward, which was the way he typically walked. Even after seven years of school attendance as regular as the rise of the sun, he moved through his days in defense mode, erecting an invisible but effective barrier between him and the rest of the student body. He had friends, just not in school.

Here in this hallway and in the classes he forced himself to attend were the kids he'd known all his life, kids whose parents made their lunches before school or gave them money to buy burgers. Kids who recognized the clothes on his back as once being theirs. Granted, there were students from neighboring areas, too, and they hadn't known at first that three quarters of his family had prison records a mile long. But news like that traveled fast.

Gus figured it was easier to socialize outside of school. He wasn't here to make friends, anyway. He intended to be the first person in his family to get a high school diploma, which would also make him the first person in his family not to be a total screwup.

Other than his grades, there was only one thing in this whole place that mattered to him.

As he ambled alongside the wall of lockers, he allowed himself to look for Lilah, spying her just as he reached his own cubby.

She stood in front of hers, surrounded by a group of girls, as she usually was. Gus made a quick half turn and deftly whirled his combination lock. All the while, though, he covertly glanced at Lilah, impatient until he saw what he was waiting for....

With one arm full of the glamour and movie magazines she routinely carted to school, Lilah slipped her other arm behind her. Resting the back of her hand against a soft blue sweater whose color matched the spring sky, she opened and closed her fist three times.

I see you. I miss you. I love you.

It was the signal they'd devised almost two years ago, when they'd first started seeing each other as more than friends.

Gus raised two fingers to his temple and rubbed them up and down, also three times.

Miss you. Want you—now. Love you, too.

He saw Lilah smile and offer a tiny head nod that had nothing to do with the conversation she was in.

The "want you" part of their secret signs was a more recent inclusion. Even after he and Lilah had started experimenting with touches and kisses that were anything but platonic, he'd tried hard to do the right thing. But a year and a half of heavy petting had been bound to lead somewhere. He'd lost his virginity at fourteen, with a girl who'd been three years older than he and who had taught him plenty. He'd known all along what to do with Lilah…and for her, shyness had not kept him at bay.

Respect had. Respect for her Uncle Harmon and respect for her. She was his golden girl. The one person other than her uncle in this hayseed town who knew him at all.

Pushing up on the slip handle, Gus opened the steel door to his locker and saw it immediately: Lilah's gift. It was hell trying not to grin as he reached in to touch the waxy petals of a white gardenia.

She'd left something in his locker every day since that afternoon in the storeroom of the jail. First it had been food—a sandwich, an apple and a donut from the bakery on Main Street, all tucked into a brown paper bag on which she'd written his name and the admonishment *Just eat it.*

It was the first time charity hadn't felt like condescension.

Gus wanted to turn, acknowledge the flower, but one of Lilah's good friends, a fellow cheerleader on the school's varsity squad, bounded up to grab her arm.

"Come on, let's go. We've got to eat quick. I want to try a couple of new hairstyles for the prom."

"We can do that after school," Lilah protested, her laughter a series of husky musical notes that forever set her apart from her peers. And made Gus's blood rush.

"I don't want to wait. There's a French braid in *Soap Opera Hairstyles* this month that uses pearl stick pins, so if we like that style, we've got to get the pearls…." Still chattering, Cathie Lyn linked her arm with Lilah's and led her down the hall toward the lunch area.

Cathie Lyn had spoken as if Lilah, too, were attending the senior prom. A logical conclusion, but Gus knew better.

Covertly glancing after her, he watched her drop a magazine, turn and bend down to pick it up, just so she could give him a wink.

He stuck his head farther into his locker and smiled as Lilah left the hallway. There were times when keeping their relationship a secret from everyone heightened the intensity of their feelings. Then there were times, like today, when all he wanted was to take Lilah's hand, announce that she was having lunch with him and find someplace to be alone with her to drink in the remaining time they had together before graduation.

He couldn't wait to get out of here, away from Kalamoose, but he and Lilah needed to make serious plans. He wanted them to begin someplace new. Somewhere his past wouldn't matter, and his family's mistakes wouldn't haunt him.

He wanted to walk with his arm around his girl, in

full view of everyone and not worry that someone might think less of her for being with him.

The white gardenia reminded him that he knew what Cathie Lyn and the others did not: Lilah wasn't going to the senior prom. She'd agreed to spend the night with him.

The plan was for Gus to borrow a car from one of the guys he occasionally worked with during haying season. Lilah would put on her prom dress and leave the house, supposedly to meet at a friend's house to wait for their dates. Instead, she'd meet him on Elk Street in front of the old cemetery. Then they'd drive into Minot and go to a restaurant and dance club Gus had heard about. He'd been eating bologna for two months to save the money for decent clothes and the dinner bill in the hope that she'd ditch the prom and go with him instead.

What she didn't know was that at the end of the night, he was going to ask her to marry him.

He didn't intend for them to marry right away. Hell, no. He wanted to have something to offer her, including a decent ring. But he knew they were headed in that direction. The right direction.

The gardenia looked waxy-white and pure as rain as it sat atop a battered textbook and a sweatshirt that needed washing. He reached out to touch it one more time, then closed the locker and headed down the hallway, nearly empty as the lunch period progressed.

When he reached the end of the hall, he paused briefly, unsure of where to go. The senior tables, which were located behind the school library rather than the cafeteria—where the other kids ate and where the aromas of hamburger, spaghetti and frying potatoes seemed ever present—would be crowded for twenty more minutes, at least. Gus almost never ate at either set of tables. He used his lunchtime to study or to hit the track for a run before his afternoon classes.

Now, as he stepped into the late May sunshine, he blinked, wondering at the curdled-milk feeling inside him.

An apple tree stood a few feet from the rear of the building, its roots spreading in gnarled fingers above the ground and making the area below the tree an inhospitable location, even to seek refuge from a glaring sun. The tree had been planted years ago as an experiment and some said it hadn't sent its roots deep into the ground because it knew it didn't belong in North Dakota. Gus figured that made him and the tree kindred spirits. When the weather was decent, and sometimes when it wasn't, he settled himself atop the woody bumps and ate his lunch in peace.

Today his steps were slow, and all he could think was that he was walking in the opposite direction from where Lilah sat with her friends.

Squinting in the too-bright sun, he took a few more paces toward his favorite spot, but each step made his gut ache worse. He'd eaten his lunch alone too many times to be bothered about it. Early on in freshman year a few kids had attempted to befriend him. But always the specter of his family and his home stopped him from getting close.

"Why don't your relatives work?" "How do you live without electricity?" "Is it true that both your parents were in prison?" The thought of such questions made him keep to himself. The only people he'd ever let in were Harm and Lilah Owens. And then only because they refused to heed his invisible sign: Warning, Keep Out.

Once again he pictured the gardenia, floating atop his books and his sweatshirt, beauty that turned a ratty locker into something special, and all at once he realized what bothered him so badly today.

He shouldn't have asked Lilah to go out with him rather than attend her prom.

Fitting in at school meant a lot to her. She liked to be the center of attention, whereas he preferred as little attention as possible. The thought of attending a dance with her, where all eyes would be on him and the belle of the ball, had always been as appealing to him as sleeping outdoors in February.

Now that school was almost out, maybe it was time to stop hiding. For her sake. She was the one great thing in his life. Perhaps taking her to the prom would be a way to prove he could be the man she needed. If their relationship was no longer secret, he could also show Harm he was serious about saving money, giving Lilah a good life.

Gus looked at the sky, high and blue, and knew that with Lilah there was no ceiling on the possibilities for his life. They'd find a different place, a better place to make their home. And he'd never give her a single reason to regret that she had faith in him.

Gus stopped walking. He turned, knowing for certain now where he was headed—the senior lunch tables.

With each step he took toward Lilah, some of the tension eased inside him. He wouldn't talk to her, couldn't "out" them; that was a decision they had to make together. He just wanted to be near her, see her, feel her love soothe the unrest inside him.

Gus circled around to the west side of the library, where he could approach the lunch tables from behind a high concrete block wall that gave him the opportunity to hear Lilah before he saw her.

"I'm telling you what Hal Birkner is telling everyone else." Brandi Kell's voice carried easily over the wall, alerting Gus to where Lilah and her group were sitting. Careful to lock his features into a casual expression, he anticipated her surprise when he walked into view.

"Well, it's ridiculous." Vivian Cheney, another of the varsity cheerleaders, spoke with clear disdain. "Lilah would *never* do that. She cares about her reputation."

Gus smiled. Must be an interesting conversation.

"If she cares about her reputation," replied Brandi, "then she'll take, like, an actual *date* to the prom. Hello? Earth to Lilah? You haven't gone out with anyone since you and Hal broke up two years ago. Now he's telling everyone he saw Gus Hoffman in the Dairy Queen parking lot, lip-locked with a blond who looked just like you. This rumor isn't going to just go away."

Gus halted so suddenly that he stumbled against the wall.

He heard the nervous laugh in Lilah's voice. "Well, for two years people have been saying Uncle Harm has turned into such a religious zealot he won't let any of us date. I guess they'll believe what they want to, anyway."

"You are *so* naive. People are going to believe whatever's juicier. If Hal Birkner tells them he saw you making out with Gus, they'll *want* to believe that. Oh, my God, Li!" Gus heard the note of emergency in Vivian's voice. "His mother's a drunk and his grandfather creeps behind Ernie's Diner all afternoon, waiting for the garbage to be dumped. That's where his family does their shopping."

It was an old "joke" that held more than a kernel of truth. Gus hadn't heard anyone talk about his grandfather in a long while, though, and was surprised at the jagged sensation the talk still stirred. He felt a rush of protectiveness that came as swift and fierce as his anger. The old man was too arthritic to hang out behind Ernie's these days, but Gus didn't doubt he brought garbage home from somewhere. Working had never been a choice.

When Lilah didn't respond, Brandi's voice rose above the wall, raspy, shocked and serious all at once. "*Were* you with Gus Hoffman in Minot? I know your uncle made you hang out with him when you were younger, but—"

"You'd never live it down," Cathie Lyn cut in, her voice holding true concern. "This town is small, and no one ever forgets anything. You haven't really been dating him, have you? Lilah, have you?"

They waited. Gus waited.

Then the answer came, low and strained. "No, of course not."

The light dimmed before Gus's eyes. Pain stabbed him, an enemy attacking from the inside out. Wincing against the angry beat of his heart, he listened to her friend's relief, to Lilah's silence, for as long as he could stand it.

He stepped around the edge of the wall, his muscles so tight he felt like a tin soldier, and ground out, "Hell no, we're not dating. She just talked to me so her uncle wouldn't cut off her allowance. The Chokecherry Princess stopped making nice to me as soon as her uncle said she could find a new charity project. Isn't that right, your highness?"

Rage nearly choked him, and he suspected he'd hate himself tomorrow for not staying out of sight and confronting Lilah later, when they were alone.

His appearance had stunned all the girls into hushed stares. Gus loathed the desperate hope inside him that waited for some response other than the stricken look on Lilah's face.

And then he saw it: a shift in her expression. Not the one he was looking for, but a silent communication that told him everything. Her eyes pleaded with him to say no more.

She wasn't going to come clean. She wasn't going to defend him in any way.

He wished he didn't need it. Wished he didn't crave her strength and her loyalty.

In the end, he walked away without another word, because he was afraid to stay, afraid to say any more. Her silence had the power to turn his love to hate, and it happened so easily he actually felt afraid.

Chapter Seven

"Harm gave me the pocket watch the week I turned eighteen," he told Lilah now, remembering his own guilt when the older man had pressed the watch into his hands with the comment that he was proud of Gus for making the most of his life.

I'm making out with your niece, he'd thought, guilty for the sneaking and for lying by omission.

Gus also remembered his fear that if Harm had discovered the truth, he would have felt suspicion and loathing rather than pride.

And yet, that day near the lunch tables Gus had been ready to risk it. He'd have gone to the prom with her, made an effort with the kids who had ridiculed him for years.

He'd have risked anything for Lilah, even the opinion of the only man who had ever guided him, ever cared.

His good sense had never been worth a plugged nickel when she was around.

"Doesn't seem like we'll have a need to see each other again, Lilah." He controlled his anger enough to sound almost philosophical. "I don't own anything else of Harm's, and you don't have anything I want."

There it was again—the wince of pain she couldn't completely conceal. As before, he felt no better, even though his arrow had hit its mark.

When she rallied, he had to check his admiration.

"It's a small town, Gus. We're bound to run into each other."

He shrugged. "Accidents happen. But I won't seek you out again while you're here. And somehow I doubt Ernie's is your usual style."

Her eyes widened. "Are you telling me to stay away from the diner?"

Gus gritted his teeth. "No. I'm—" What *was* he doing, besides prolonging this conversation? "Eat where you damn well please."

Turning, he strode into the night, beneath the same stars that watched him race from her door years ago.

Getting into the car he'd parked on the other side of the road, he promised himself he would not look back at the house.

He broke that vow as soon as he made it, glancing

over to see Lilah, a halo of golden light silhouetting her in the doorway as she watched him pull away.

Same as always.

Cinnamon and butter, vanilla and chocolate—the aromas swirled around Lilah, but all she wanted was coffee. Lots of coffee. Hold the milk, hold the sugar; she required a high-octane jolt to the adrenals.

She was tired.

No. *Tired* was a normal feeling. She felt like a dead woman walking. Or, if not walking, propped up on a wrought iron chair, slurping her first cup of the morning in Mamie's Bakery.

"Can I have another doughnut? I want one of those cinnamon-apple things," Bree asked with her mouth still full of doughnut number one, a cream-filled cruller.

Bree's feet, which hardly ever stopped jiggling, were rhythmically kicking the small table at which she and Lilah sat. The thumping seemed to beat in cadence with the pounding in Lilah's head.

Two weeks had passed since she'd spoken to Gus in the doorway of her sister's home. She hadn't visited Ernie's since her first night back in town. She bought her gas in the next town over, and she hadn't run into Gus anywhere else.

So far, okay.

Lilah had also gotten a job since the night she'd spoken to Gus. A waitstaff position at a coffee shop in Minot, an hour away. She worked the graveyard shift, so she was gone only when Bree was asleep and Sara was available. She'd been lucky to get the work, though the drive and the hours and the cigarette smoke from the regulars who frequented the run-down establishment were killing her.

Small-town, central North Dakota was not exactly a hotbed of employment. After scouring the want ads, which hadn't taken long as there'd only been two pages to begin with, she'd grabbed the first paying gig she'd been offered. Her only thought had been to make enough money to keep Bree fed until she could figure out what came next.

Looking at Bree now, at the twitchy restlessness that seemed to characterize the eleven-year-old of late, guilt flowed through Lilah, more powerful than the caffeine that had yet to take effect.

"I think," she said, trying to imagine how Grace would have answered her daughter's request, "that if you have any more sugar, Mamie will have to scrape you off the ceiling. Drink your milk. The cows are local."

Bree wrinkled her nose. "Eww, gross. Like I want to think about *that.*"

"What? That cows are raised where we can see them? That they're allowed to graze freely and are milked humanely?"

"Whatever! I don't want to think about *udders.*"

Laughter rose above Lilah's fatigue. The past two weeks had been a kind of dance between her and Bree. They never mentioned Grace…well, Lilah had, but Bree refused to talk about her mother. She asked lots of questions, though, about what it was like to grow up in North Dakota, and about why Lilah left and about how cool did it feel to have a sister who wore a gun to work? Lilah got plenty nervous over that question and subsequently made sure Sara had a long talk with Bree about firearms safety.

The weird part—weird to Lilah, at any rate—was that Bree seemed to like it here.

She trailed Sara around the house and asked to visit her at the jail.

She rode Sara's old bike until her face was as red as the aluminum frame.

She brought home cut dahlias from Mrs. Karpoun's garden and the last of the summer berries from Henry Markham's brambles. She was getting to know the neighbors.

She still didn't love Lilah, but they were getting along…better.

"Are you almost done?" she asked her guardian now, eyeing the newspaper Lilah had folded on the table. Lilah continued to comb the want ads every morning on the very slim chance something new might pop up. "If I can't have another doughnut, I want to ride my bike. It's *bor*-ing in here."

"Shh." Lilah leaned forward, nearly knocking over her coffee cup. "You don't want to offend Mamie. She's very proud of her new book selection." Lilah nodded toward a tall bookcase, crammed with paperbacks from Mamie's personal collection. "Maybe she has the latest Harry Potter."

"Been there." Bree kicked the table harder, a largely unconscious act, Lilah was sure, but the sound made her wince as the pounding in her head increased exponentially.

"I want to look at this last column of want ads, so maybe you could find something worth your reading minutes."

"You talk weird." Bree slid around on her chair, resting her arms along the back, choosing to gaze aimlessly around the small bakery rather than follow Lilah's suggestion. "What's wrong with the job you've got?" she asked after a minute.

"I hardly know where to start," Lilah mumbled, putting a big X through one of the ads she'd called last week: cocktail waitress at a place called Dive Bomb, which summed up her professional life at the moment.

Tucking the pen behind her ear, she spoke to Bree's slender back. "My job is an hour drive each way, and the shift is terrible. I don't like being that far away from you. If you needed something I wouldn't be able to get to you right away."

Bree was still for a moment then shrugged her narrow shoulders. "I'm not a baby."

Lilah nodded. "Well, I could use a lot more money than I'm making now, too."

"How long are we staying here?"

"I'm not sure," she responded carefully. "I'm not exactly certain yet what our plans are."

Bree did look over her shoulder then. "Are you ever going to be an actress again? My mom said you did plays and TV and stuff. How come I've never seen you in anything?"

Cut to the chase, kid. It wasn't the first time Lilah had been posed that question, though often it had been couched in positives: *"Oh, you're an actress. Well, you're certainly pretty enough. Where can we see you?"*

Back then she'd offered her headshot smile and answered, "Be sure to tune into *Days of our Lives* this week. There's going to be a surprise earthquake in Salem. I'll be the third corpse from the left as you face your TV screen."

At twenty-two that response had been funny. Now that she was knocking on the door of thirty, the joke had grown weary.

"I've done a few things," she said carefully, knowing she'd reached a crossroads.

Frankly, she wanted to lie to Bree, to pad her resume so the eleven-year-old wouldn't realize that after over a decade in Los Angeles, Lilah had accomplished pretty much zilch, theatrically speaking. For years, she'd talked up her smallest under-five role on TV, the tiniest part in some destined-to-remain-unknown play, making everything seem bigger and better than it actually was. It made her feel better to think that other people still believed she was "on her way."

Yeah, on my way to total obscurity. And possibly food stamps.

Lilah ran unmanicured fingers through the hair she'd always kept long and full and shining.

Her fibs, the hair she'd paid the best Beverly Drive stylists to highlight at regularly scheduled appointments, her always careful makeup—those were all tactics to hide the truth. And the truth was that she'd never been good enough to pick her career up off the ground.

The truth was that the qualities that had made her a standout in Kalamoose made her a dime-a-dozen actress in Hollywood.

She'd been hiding the facts for years, hiding them even from herself. Up to now, reality had been palatable only when viewed through the lens of dreams. In her daydreams, there was always the hope that her bright, success-filled future was right around the corner.

Lilah looked at Bree, eleven and already facing uncertainties no child should have to deal with. The last thing the poor kid needed to hear right now was that her life was in the hands of one long-in-the-tooth starlet who didn't know the first thing about kids, college funds or 401(k)s. Lilah knew she should sit down soon with Bree to discuss their future together, to discuss so many things; but first she wanted to be able to present a little evidence, at least, that she might make a decent mother.

Mother.

The very word made her quiver.

The universe better have a plan, she thought, *because saddling this kid with me looks like poor management.*

She considered mentioning the possible role in the small-budget independent comedy a friend of hers from acting class was producing. Maybe that would reassure

Bree that she hadn't been put in the hands of a total screwup.

But if that movie was never made—or it was made without her—what would she tell Bree next? Nine-tenths of a struggling actress's job was to *appear* successful when she wasn't. The effort had become exhausting.

When the pounding in her head increased, Lilah dug into the pocket of her jeans for one of the ibuprofen she tucked there each morning.

Grace had been the blessed one. She'd been a simple woman, worked in pharmaceutical sales…nothing very glamorous about that. Her name had never been featured on a marquee. She'd never seen her picture in a magazine, and she'd never needed to. She'd known who she was. Only the people who had known her would remember her name. But Bree had loved her completely.

Climbing into bed with her mother every night during those final weeks, Bree had curled in the circle of Grace's too-thin arms, ignoring the bruises the dialysis had left, ignoring the unmistakable aroma of illness, ignoring everything but the mother-daughter need to hold on.

And, ignoring her own pain, Grace had settled Bree against her breast each night, stroking her hair slowly… so slowly…as if they'd had all the time in the world.

Lilah looked across the table at Bree's profile. There was a furrow most of the time now between her eyebrows. She'd taken to chewing the inside of her bottom lip, like Lilah.

How could she mother this child? What could she—a woman who had faked most of her life for the past ten years—give to a child who needed something real and lasting?

"Your mother was a better person than I've ever been," she began, capturing Bree's attention. "She was smarter and wiser. You know, I was only seventeen when I first met her, and she was twenty-nine, the same age I am now. But she owned her own home already. She always seemed to know where she was going. She wanted a family more than anything."

Bree lowered her gaze to the floor, but she didn't turn completely away. "But she couldn't have kids."

"No."

"So she adopted me." The mumbled statement emerged half sure and proud and half like a question.

"Yes." Lilah felt her throat tighten. "She told me she knew the moment she saw you that God had made you for each other."

Bree nodded. "I know," she said. The voice of one who had been told she was loved, wanted, needed on more than one occasion. "Were you there when my mom brought me home? I heard the story lots of times, but she never said you were there."

"No." Lilah tried to keep her voice calm and assured. "I wasn't there that day. But she told me about it…how happy she was."

Bree recommenced kicking the chair. Her voice was so low Lilah had to lean forward to make out the words.

"Do you think my mom can see me, or maybe…hear me if I talk to her?"

Lilah's heart squeezed until she could hardly breathe. "Both. I think she does both." Her hand crept halfway across the table toward Bree's, but Bree's hands were now clasped tightly on her lap. Lilah settled for using words to get closer. "I told her I didn't know anything about being a parent. You know what she said? She said I wouldn't be alone, because she'd be watching over us. She said part of her spirit would stay and help us through."

She paused a moment, praying her words would help bring Bree closer rather than push the girl further away, then confessed, "I talk to Grace sometimes…when I'm confused. At night, especially. I ask her to help me learn how to talk to you."

When Bree raised her head, Lilah found herself looking into a gaze that met hers straight on, devoid of the usual hostility.

Lilah held her breath, heart thumping heavily as she wondered whether today would mark a true turning point in their relationship. And if it did, how long before she could give Bree the letter Grace had left for her?

Grace had written a final note to her daughter, but she'd asked that Lilah wait to share it until Bree could turn easily to Lilah for comfort. They weren't there yet, heaven knew.

Before the moment proved to be a true transformation, the bell on the bakery door jingled and a young boy walked in. Bree looked over immediately, and whatever intimacy had been generated quickly dissipated.

A year or two older than her, the boy wore clean blue jeans, a green T-shirt and an expression of simple goodwill as he glanced around the bakery. He smiled at Bree, which brought a flush of pink to her cheeks.

The boy's features were clearly Lakota. His eyes were dark and shining, his skin tanned to a beautiful cinnamon shade. Carrying a woven basket Lilah recognized immediately as a Native American handicraft, he nodded at her and Bree as he passed by their table.

Greeting Mamie's other two customers by name, he proceeded around the counter to the open side of the pastry case.

Mamie was in the back of the store, but that didn't stop the young man from reaching into the case to withdraw a number of plump pastries to fill his basket.

When the proprietress returned to the front, wiping her hands with a food-stained towel, she put a grandmotherly hand on the boy's shoulder.

"Elan, you're early. I've got the sandwiches almost done."

"Hi, Mamie." He gave her a big, straight-toothed grin that instantly made him cover material for *Teen Beat* magazine. "Dad's going to meet me here. He's driving me to my deliveries today and then we're heading to Minot to shop for school."

Mamie smiled approvingly. "I'll hurry then. You take a Danish for yourself, why don't you? The cherry's the best I've ever made."

"You say that every day."

"It's true every day." Mamie spoke with the singsong lilt characteristic of folks who'd been born and raised in small-town North Dakota and had never left.

Bree seemed mesmerized, so Lilah watched, too, as Mamie stuffed her towel between the string of her apron and the soft roll of her stomach then returned to the back of the store. Left on his own, Elan dug into his pocket for change then rang up the sale of his cherry Danish and put the money in the register. Only then did he select one of the fat, iced pastries for himself.

Lilah nodded. Honest. Industrious, too. He clearly delivered sandwiches and baked goods for Mamie. Though Lilah questioned the need for such a service in Kalamoose in the summer, she figured that during the winter he could make decent pocket money delivering to seniors and others who didn't want to brave the snow for their morning coffee and bear claw.

Someone was raising the young man with a work ethic. Would she be able to do the same for Bree?

Raising her rapidly cooling coffee to her lips, Lilah wondered what Elan was like at home, whether he had siblings and how his parents had acted to shape his disposition. What she needed was a parenting mentor.

Deep in thought, and very aware that Bree was fascinated by the young Lakota boy, she nearly dropped her mug when the door to the bakery opened again and Gus walked in.

Gus faltered only briefly when he saw her. They'd successfully avoided each other for two weeks.

He nodded in acknowledgment of her presence, but said nothing as he proceeded to the counter. Once again, he was dressed in Kalamoose haute couture—a gray-green suit, pale shirt and silver tie.

Elan was just coming around the counter with his snack. He looked at Gus and grinned. "Mamie says these are her best cherry Danishes yet. Want one, Dad?"

Chapter Eight

Coffee shot through Lilah's nose.

When she began a choking fit, Bree turned to stare at her, and Lilah grabbed a paper napkin to stifle as much of the sound as she could.

Stunned, not even sure she'd absolutely heard correctly, she gaped blatantly as Gus shook his head at the boy.

"After pancakes and syrup this morning?" he asked, humor tingeing his voice. "I think you have to be twelve to digest that much sugar in a couple of hours."

Lilah latched immediately on to the information that Elan was twelve. In her buzzing brain she did the math.

If Elan was twelve, and Gus had been a father for that many years... She almost choked again.

He'd been seventeen when Elan's mother had become pregnant. Which meant—

Her lungs seemed to stop working.

Gus had cheated on her.

Even as he'd told her he loved her, *showed* her he loved her, and even while he'd blamed her for not admitting to their relationship, he had been with another girl.

The lying, manipulative—

He smiled at his son, and Lilah watched them both ease into iron-backed chairs at a round table for two. Elan ate his pastry while they waited for Mamie to bring out the sandwiches she was making.

Lilah wanted to march over to Gus's table and demand answers to the questions shouting in her head, but Bree was watching them, too. She couldn't confront Gus in front of Bree and Elan.

She shouldn't do it at all. Not until she'd had time to think.

"Come on, Bree, let's get out of here."

The girl turned to pick up her milk and started sucking it slowly through a red-striped straw. "I'm not finished," she muttered, once again kicking the chair while she glanced around at Gus and his son.

"You can finish it on the walk home." Quickly stuffing her pen and the want ads into her purse, Lilah stood.

Bree ignored her.

Lilah's lips barely moved as she ordered, "Get your tush out of the chair and follow me!"

Without waiting, she turned and fled the bakery,

making Mamie's bells clank too hard against the glass door and hoping Bree would follow without comment.

When the doorbells jingled again behind her and Bree appeared, Lilah muttered, "Thank you," then started walking. Silently, Bree fell into step beside her.

She was twenty-nine; since the age of seventeen she'd carried more than her fair share of guilt and shame for hurting Gus.

The rat bastard.

The heels of her sandals slapped against the sidewalk. She felt Bree's confusion, but couldn't relieve it. There were still secrets to be kept.

At almost thirty years old, Lilah finally realized the price of lies and evasions; not only did they put distance between her and the people from whom she'd hidden the truth, but ultimately dishonesty made her a stranger to herself.

Her steps slowed a bit, became softer, as first awareness and then surrender settled in.

Truth. She'd avoided it like the plague. Feared it. Dreaded the anger and disappointment it would raise. Now she sensed it was the only thing that would save her…and save Bree, too. It was time to clear up the past.

Wishing she could take Bree's hand, say, "Trust me," tell her that everything was going to turn out okay and actually be believable, Lilah settled for silently vowing to give Bree a reason to believe.

She was going to lay the pieces of her life out where

she could see them. The only place to start was with the man back at the bakery.

A couple of weeks earlier, Bree had struck up an acquaintance with Rosie Becker, who drove the bookmobile that came to Kalamoose on Mondays, Wednesdays and Fridays. Generally Rosie pulled up to 4th and C streets at 11:00 a.m., stayed through the lunch hour and, if there was interest, for an hour beyond that. For the past two weeks, Bree had climbed into Rosie's van, chosen a book and remained there the entire two hours.

The first couple of times that Bree had planted herself in the roving library, Lilah had hovered close by until finally Rosie had waved her off with a chortle. "I used to sit here for three hours when Nettie was this one's age. It took the Jaws of Life to get her off my van once she discovered the Narnia series. Go on. This little gal'll be fine."

So today, Lilah dropped Bree off, told Rosie she had to run a few errands and hopped in her car. She drove first to the gas station, but eventually found Gus at the diner, going over the daily audit.

He emerged through a door adorned with a stained hand-lettered sign that read If You Work Here, Come On Back. If You Don't Work Here, Put On An Apron Then Come On Back. Though Gus now owned the diner, he'd obviously left a lot of Ernie's touches. Ernie, however, had never worn a suit to work, had probably never even owned one. Once again Lilah noted how out of place Gus looked in his classically cut designer ensemble.

She shook her head as he approached the register, where she stood, waiting for him. "You do clean up well, Gus." She tilted her head at him. "I'm just wondering what happened to the boy whose clothes used to scream, 'Bite me' instead of 'Hire me'?"

At twenty past eleven, the regular lunch crowd at Ernie's consisted mostly of retired farmers and creamery employees who had been bellying up to this same counter for years. More than a couple of graying eyebrows rose at Lilah's comment.

Gus acknowledged her with a small smile. "You answered your own question. I was a boy then."

His gaze traveled over the sleeveless denim vest and matching skirt she'd chosen for this meeting. Even her three-inch high sandals had denim straps. She was the Melrose Avenue version of Daisy Duke, hip and sexy, and she'd dressed that way deliberately to give herself confidence. She'd even arranged her long hair in a tousled upsweep to hide as much of her darker roots as possible.

"I see *you* still favor the same type of wardrobe that you did in high school, Lilah," he drawled, careful diction matching his careful appearance.

She felt the anger she'd been riding since this morning carry her further into prickly territory. "Yes, I'm consistent that way. Unfortunately, consistency doesn't seem to be *your* forte, does it?"

His eyes and jaw grew hard. Several pairs of elderly ears seemed to stretch in their direction, and Gus placed a hand beneath Lilah's bare elbow. "Would you care to see my office, Miss Owens? I've redecorated." He began leading her in that direction before she consented.

"Love to," she bit out, marching along beside him with an agenda of her own.

They walked through a kitchen staffed mostly by young people Lilah didn't know, though she did glimpse Gloria, a waitress who had worked here so long some people said only God remembered when she'd started.

Spotting Lilah with her new boss, Gloria waved a be-ringed hand before lining three hot plates up on her left arm, grabbing a fourth plate with her right hand and gliding smoothly out of the kitchen. *The mark of a waitress who's been serving tables most of her days,* Lilah noted. Gloria's life must have held few surprises at this point.

On the other hand, Gus's office was a complete shock. Lilah was certain that when the small space had been Ernie's, it had looked nothing like it did now.

Surrounded by stucco on four sides, the space could have been claustrophobic. Gus had painted it a beautiful, peaceful sage green, however, and had hung black-and-white photos of Lakota elders around the room. There were also weavings in coordinating earth tones and a calm-inducing fountain on the far edge of the neatly organized glass-topped desk.

Lilah stood just inside the door and wagged her head. "Okay, you got me. Why *would* a person completely redecorate an office no one is going to see, but not bother to remodel a broken-down restaurant that still calls Seven-Up the Un-Cola?"

Gus pulled her into the office and shut the door. "Not everyone cares about what others will see, Lilah. Integrity is about staying true to what has meaning for you."

Integrity, huh?

Stalking to the sleek, black leather desk chair, she plopped herself down, crossed her long legs and arms and glared at Gus. "You're all morals and ideals when it's convenient, aren't you? You want to talk about integrity? Start with twelve years ago. No—" She held up a hand. "Start with twelve years *and nine months ago.* Enlighten me, Gus, as to what you were doing around that time. Other than luring an *innocent* teenage girl to your bed on the pretext that you were in love with her. *Only* her."

Now that, she thought, swinging one strappy high heel, *is getting to the point.*

"Am I supposed to have any idea what you're talking about?"

"Your son? The twelve-year-old you were with in the bakery this morning?" To Gus's astonished look, she added, "Yeah, that's right. I heard you refer to his age. I did the math." She raised a palm. "Not that I was listening in. It's a very small bakery."

Recovering from the initial surprise, Gus shook his head with a smile. "What's your point, Lilah?"

Evasive, she noted, enjoying the idea that when she

finished cataloging his faults she would stop noticing his beautiful jawline.

Rising from the chair, she knew her fury was a little too fresh, her pain too raw. She shouldn't have confronted him until she'd had time to cool off, but she'd never been good at waiting.

Taking two steps forward, she stood with all the poise of which she was capable. "My point is that I have felt guilty—no, I have felt sick and ashamed—for over a decade because I denied loving you when my friends confronted me. You, on the other hand—are a conniving snake. You acted hurt and abused even though you knew you'd been cheating on me all along. I thought I'd ruined your life!"

Gus appeared fascinated by everything she said, but reacted with infuriating control, resembling a mountain—calm and immovable in the face of angry elements.

"Are you sorry you didn't ruin my life?"

Lilah's knuckles dug into her hips. "Of course not. That's not even the point. The point is you're a cheat. And all these years you let me believe that I was the skunk in our relationship."

He shrugged. "If the stripe fits."

Lilah brought one balled fist away from her hip, looking as if she was going to wallop him, which she wouldn't have, though it was a gratifying picture in her head. He narrowed his eyes dangerously.

"You've jumped to two very big conclusions, Lilah. And they're leading you far afield of the truth."

"How's that?"

"You've assumed Elan is my biological son, and you've assumed I'm a liar, neither of which is true."

Gus saw the troubled uncertainty in Lilah's eyes. For a moment it replaced the pain and spitting anger with which she'd walked into his establishment.

Nothing could have prepared him for the peace that settled his spirit when he realized how upset, how genuinely wounded she was by the thought of him with another girl. For the first time in years he could stop wondering whether their love had been one-sided. He'd needed the knowledge that she'd loved him the way a dying man needs absolution.

He should let it go now. Drop it. He had a present that needed his attention; he had a wife and family in his future. Lilah Owens could only impede that.

"What do you mean he's not your 'biological' son? In the bakery he called you, 'Dad.'"

"I'm Elan's foster father. He calls me Dad, and I'm hoping to adopt him. After Karen and I are married."

That stopped her. Her forehead pinched as if she had a migraine coming on.

Then she realized Elan was not proof she'd been cheated on, but rather proof that Gus had moved on with life.

"I just made a total fool of myself." Embarrassment made her pulse jump at the base of her neck.

That and the tinge of red on her cheeks tugged at Gus,

chinking away at the armor he'd never been very good at maintaining where she was concerned.

"I'm not going to tell anyone," he said, noticing for the first time that beneath the humiliated blush, her skin looked sallow. There were faint lavender-gray shadows beneath her eyes and her collarbone was too prominent.

"What have you been doing for the past two weeks?" he asked. "You look like hell."

"Well, thank you. After making a total idiot of myself, it's nice to hear that I also look awful." She hitched her purse higher on her shoulder, preparing to leave. "In Los Angeles I'd need therapy for months after a day like today."

Self-deprecating humor was not a trait he recalled seeing in her before. It was hard not to smile.

"When was the last time you had a decent meal? You're not on some kind of Hollywood wheatgrass and brown rice diet, are you?"

"Hardly," she scoffed. "I prefer breakfast bars and diet soda." She patted a hip. "Gotta get a little sweet taste in while I'm whittling off the pounds."

Gus scowled, wondering how much truth there was to the notion that she was perpetually on a diet.

He knew she hadn't worked much as an actress, not on TV or film. He'd checked the Internet Movie Database more times than he'd ever admit. He also knew she'd worked hard to project the image of a successful starlet. Photos of her were all over Kalamoose. In Mamie's bakery...on the walls at Ernie's...even at the tavern.

Understanding Lilah's need to stand out, to be loved not by one but by many, he could easily guess that she'd toned, teased and dieted her way through Hollywood. He looked at her now—way too thin and with the weary too-young-to-be-this-fatigued look that seemed to plague some actresses and models. Who looked out for her in L.A.? Were there people in her life who would tell her the truth?

Whoa, he thought. *None of your business. Don't even go there.*

Spinning on his heel, he strode to the office door and yanked it open. Then he leaned out and called to his line cook. "Dirk, I need a burger—no onions, extra tomato— and fries, very crisp. Dinner salad with Thousand Island. And ask Gloria to make a chocolate shake, would you?"

When he turned back toward Lilah, she was regarding him with a raised eyebrow. "Hungry?" she asked.

"It's for you."

"Me? I'm not—"

"You look like you're starving, so don't argue. You don't have the kind of body that looks right waifish, or whatever the hell they call it."

"I'm not—"

Ignoring her, he leaned out the door again. "Dirk, add an order of onion rings." He faced Lilah again. "Those are for me. I *might* share."

He knew he positively shouldn't have said that. When the meal came, he'd leave her to eat it in peace. Alone. Swear to God.

* * *

It took only a second or two for Lilah to realize that he'd ordered her meal exactly the way she used to, right down to the extra-crisp fries.

For a moment she felt sixteen. Sixteen and known best by the boy she loved.

Once, that warm, sheltering feeling had gone with her wherever she went. It had been absent for a long time.

There had been nights in Los Angeles when she'd lain in bed after a botched audition or a particularly grueling shift at the restaurant and tried to remember that feeling: the sense that somewhere there was someone who was thinking of her while she thought of him.

She and Gus didn't know each other anymore. He remembered her favorite junk-food meal from when she was sixteen, but he didn't know about so many things that had happened since he saw her last.

"Thank you for the offer, but I'd better get going—"

"You can take a few minutes to sit down and eat. You look—"

"You already told me how I look." She frowned at him. "I look tired because I'm working graveyard at the Pie 'n' Burger in Minot. You'd be frayed around the edges, too, if you left the house at midnight so you could serve chili to insomniacs."

Disapproval filled Gus's expression when he demanded, "Why did you take a job like that?"

"Uh…it pays?" She favored him with a think-about-it look. "This is central North Dakota, Gus. My options were limited."

"You're broke."

"Financially challenged," she quipped, but changed her tack when his scowl deepened. "I'm kidding. I'm *fine*. I have a nice nest egg from my acting, and there'll be plenty more jobs when I get back to L.A. I just don't like to spend all my savings, you know?"

"Minot's over an hour away. What are you driving? The junker you were in when you first pulled up to the gas station?"

"She is not a junker! She's a…classic. And she's very reliable."

"The car's a heap and you shouldn't be driving those roads alone in the middle of the night to begin with."

His clenched jaw put a warm, grateful tingle in her chest. She shrugged it off. "Please. I live in Los Angeles." He looked at her as if she were very naive. "I carry pepper spray."

Trying to lighten the mood and distract herself from taking his concern too personally, she asked, "Since when did you become a slave to personal safety?"

She posed the question with a smile, but he'd clearly developed a literal side.

"Since I spent eleven months in a federal penitentiary with men who preyed on women like you."

"Women like me?"

"The kind who believe pepper spray can make a foolish choice wise."

She didn't have a choice about whether to work, but decided not to say so. Instead, she allowed his mention of prison to hover between them—an elephant that no one wanted to mention was in the room.

She'd rushed to him after he'd been put in jail, but that was the last time they'd seen each other or spoken, until the present.

"I heard that you had some…trouble in jail and that you'd gone to prison." Lilah spoke haltingly, not sure there was a politic way to discuss a person's prison term. "Uncle Harm told me you fought with another… uh…"

"Inmate?" Gus hooked an eyebrow. "Yeah. He thought I ought to come to him for all my nonprescription drug needs."

"Oh. Did you have nonprescription drug needs?"

"No, that's one area of trouble I managed to avoid." He looked at her wryly. "I did fight with the pusher and some of his friends, though. I was still dealing with an anger issue. At the time I thought I was standing my ground, but the prison psychologist pointed out that walking away might have been an option."

"You saw a prison psychologist?"

"Free group therapy, once a week for eleven months."

Neither of them spoke for a moment. Lilah was thinking about the incident that had sent him to jail in the first place.

"I felt terrible about your being arrested, Gus. I felt responsible."

"You told me."

His voice was flat, and she assumed he wasn't going to be any more amenable to her apology now than he'd been the day she'd gone to see him in the jail.

He ran a hand through his hair and rolled his shoulders as if his thoughts were a physical burden. "You weren't responsible for my actions. Although I suppose I've spent an inordinate amount of time wanting to believe you were." The confession seemed to help. His gray eyes began to warm.

"Well, you did drag race with those boys because you were angry with me."

"I drag raced because they asked me," he contradicted. "That wasn't the first time I'd climbed into the driver's seat to play rebel without a cause."

That was true. She'd even stood on the sidelines once, Natalie Wood to his James Dean, and she had to admit that the speed and the danger of it all had excited her.

Still, she recalled that on the night in question he'd drag raced down the center of Main Street in a car he'd hot-wired, with a fifth of the cheapest whiskey on the seat beside him. That had been more horrifying than exciting.

"You ran the car into the front of Hertzog's Grocery because you were drunk," she pointed out. "And you drank because—"

"Because I was a reckless, pissed-off idiot. I could have killed someone that night. That was no one's fault but mine. I drank because I didn't know how to handle my anger."

"Toward me?"

He sighed. "Toward everyone, Lilah, including you." He wagged his head. "Hell, yes, I was angry at you. I'd heard you tell your friends you'd never be with someone like me, and later that night you refused to say yes when I proposed."

"I was wrong to say what I did to my friends." It had to be the tenth time, in all, that she'd apologized. She'd apologize ten more times if it helped. She still felt awful about that horrid afternoon. But... "As for the marriage proposal, the timing was a little off, don't you think? You asked me in the middle of a huge fight."

He was ready to argue, but stopped with his mouth half-open. He clamped his lips, but one corner of his lips twitched up. "You have a point."

For the first time in over a decade, they actually managed to smile at each other.

After a few quiet seconds had passed, she ventured, "I'm sorry I never came to the jail to see you after that first time."

Gus rubbed a hand over his smooth jaw. "I didn't exactly give you a reason to come back."

Neither of them would ever forget the anger or accusations at that last, painful meeting. She'd gone to the jail to tell him that she loved him still, that she truly was sorry she hadn't defended him to her friends and that she would stand by him if his case went to trial.

He hadn't thought much of the offer. With no finesse, but an abundance of rage, he'd told her he didn't want to see her again. He'd called her shallow, spat that her contest titles and her cheerleading were "trivial" and "boring." Then he'd done the worst thing he could have done to her: shaking his head with pity, Gus had told her she was a lousy actress and was kidding herself if she thought she was going to make it in L.A. She'd be a dime a dozen, he'd sneered, and she'd be alone.

His derision had felt like a fist around her heart. It had squeezed the breath out of her, strangled her confidence.

Earlier that year, he'd sat on his own in the back of the auditorium when she'd played Madge in a high school production of *Picnic*. At the curtain call, he'd stood before anyone else and applauded. Later that night he had come to the house when everyone was in bed and held her in his arms under the eaves.

With his cheek resting against her head and his lips whispering into her hair, he'd told her she was beautiful and perfect in the part. Lilah had breathed in the lilac and the moonlight and the perfect scent of Gus's skin and knew the memory of that moment would last forever.

And then in a spate of angry words, he'd taken it away. He'd stolen back the confidence his love and support had given her. That moment under the eaves had been the one perfect moment she'd had since her parents had died, the only time she'd recaptured the wholeness and security and the hope that although she wasn't as serious as Sara or as sweet as Nettie, she would be loved just as she was.

She'd fled the jail feeling lost and confused and almost as angry with him as he was with her.

Now here they were: two people who'd been alternately holding grudges and blaming themselves. Two people who still weren't done with each other.

As they stood in the silence and remembered, a change seemed to overcome Gus. The enmity that had infused his gaze since her return softened to pensiveness.

He walked to a charcoal drawing of the North Dakota prairie and looked at it as if he were gazing out a window. "Funny how much I wanted to get away from here when in my heart I knew all along I'd be back."

He turned toward her, noting her surprise. "When I said you weren't good enough to make it in Hollywood, that was a lie." The intentness in his eyes told her to listen carefully to what he was saying.

He studied her hair…her face… "I knew all along you were too good for me. Too beautiful and too big to keep for myself. I suppose that's what hurt the most— knowing my dreams never had a chance."

Lilah felt shaken by an explosion that blasted a hole in what she thought she knew.

He expelled a breath he'd been holding a long time. "I spoke out of fear as much as anger that night. I've been waiting a long while to say that to you. To tell you the truth, I wasn't sure I would." He shook his head. "Honesty. What a concept."

Lilah felt as if she might throw up. A dozen years ago she had listened to his ego instead of his heart. She had run away and changed both their lives. "Yeah," she muttered, "what a concept."

More words, a confession, hovered on her lips. Tension charged the distance between them, but for the first time in years the tension was born of something other than anger. He studied her, and she him, searching perhaps for kinder remnants of the past. Lilah's mind raced. If she knew him better, if he wasn't engaged, perhaps now would be the time to tell him about the months after she left Kalamoose, about how life had changed forever and about the decisions she had made. For years she had lived with a secret that if told could end the enmity between her and Gus...or build it to frightening proportions.

A knock on the door broke the spell between them.

Gus left her to open the door to a waitress who handed him a round tray with their lunch plates. The aroma of grilled burger, hot fries and onion rings should have been appetizing since Lilah truly hadn't managed to eat a full meal in a while. Unfortunately, her whirling mind kept her stomach turning, too.

"I can set it up on the desk," Gus offered. "Or we can go into the restaurant."

Her throat felt tight. "We?"

"Hmm." He frowned. "I was the one who said we should keep our distance, wasn't I?" He studied her, glanced at the tray. "On the other hand, those are my onion rings, so maybe just this once...?"

His lips edged into a self-mocking smile.

For years after she'd left Kalamoose, Gus's image had popped into her head spontaneously. When she'd wanted someone to talk to, when she'd accomplished something small in her career and when she hadn't—it had been his face to whom she had spoken, but his eyes she'd imagined lighting with pride or deepening with compassion.

She'd tried not to take the habit too seriously, but Gus had remained a mystery all these years—she hadn't known where he was, whether he'd met someone else or still thought about her—and unsolved mysteries were notoriously difficult to put from one's mind.

Now she knew he was engaged. He'd found someone else. One mystery solved. She sighed. Hopefully the knowledge would help her let go, to find someone else's face to talk to. She had made a lot of mistakes in her life, but fooling around with another woman's man had never been one of them.

If she stuck around for lunch, took advantage of his change in attitude to get to know him a little better, there would be no real harm. He was most assuredly off-limits now, and soon enough her secrets would have to be told. Then his gray eyes could turn colder and more accusing than she had ever seen them.

Perhaps his fiancée wouldn't mind—too much—if she stole just a few moments with Gus before the animosity returned.

Chapter Nine

Even at the height of the lunch hour, the diner was over half-empty, so taking a booth was no problem. And they still had enough privacy for Lilah to ask the questions most on her mind.

"So why the diner, Gus?" Mostly to give her hands something to do, she unwrapped a paper-covered straw and stuck it in her chocolate shake while he turned a plastic container upside down and squirted catsup onto the plate of onion rings. "Have you had food service experience?"

"No. I bought Ernie's because it's the social hub of this town."

"'Social hub'?" For the first time in weeks she laughed simply because something was funny.

His lips curved. Glancing around, he lowered his voice pointedly. "Okay, I use the term loosely." He dunked an onion ring in catsup and took a bite. "Still, other than the tavern it is the town's main gathering place."

"And this was appealing to you all of a sudden...why?"

"It wasn't sudden. I bought a sizeable piece of land a few years ago even though I knew I wouldn't be able to return for good until this year. Now I'm putting a home and a business on the property."

Lilah shook her head. It was still so hard to fathom Gus returning to Kalamoose for good, as he'd said. "What kind of business?"

"I'm building a food production plant and gift store." When her eyes widened, he visibly warmed to the topic. "We're going to carry products exclusively made in the Dakotas—Native American handicrafts, and books on the Lakota and early German settlers. Foods from classic farm and Native American recipes."

He lowered his voice a notch. "Eventually this diner will function as a tie-in to the store. The menu will feature the foods we're selling. The decor will reflect the cultural diversity of the area."

"Cultural diversity? In Kalamoose?"

"There's always been plenty of diversity. Unfortunately it was repressed instead of honored. Lakota or European, we've all left our marks."

"And you want the marks to show."

"Yes."

He was staring at her levelly, and she smiled, because in that moment she saw both his more turbulent Germanic and the more enigmatic Lakota roots. She heard the pride in his voice, but it was difficult, almost impossible, to read him when he shuttered his expression, as he did now. He waited for her response.

In truth, she was proud of him. "I've never heard anyone plan so much for this little town. It sounds like you'll create a lot of jobs."

He nodded and she glimpsed the satisfaction behind his eyes.

It sounded, too, as if he either had a lot of backers or had amassed a small fortune to put toward his new endeavor. Either way, this wasn't the dirt-poor kid whose big dream had been escape. He'd once said he would take any job he had to as long as it was in a big city.

"I don't get it, though," she confessed. "You couldn't wait to get out of here."

"No. I couldn't stand to stay. It's not the same thing."

She frowned. "You've lost me."

Gus pointed to her lunch. "Eat. Burgers and fries are only good when they're hot." He plucked the side of Thousand Island dressing from the salad he'd ordered for her and slid it over.

Dutifully, she picked up a fry, drenching it in pink dressing, the way she'd always done.

Gus waited until she'd eaten one long, crisp potato then pushed the burger her way. Rolling her eyes, she flattened the thick sandwich with both hands, dunked it in the Thousand Island as well and took a bite. It was good.

"That's a better burger than I remember," she said around a mouthful.

Gratification squared his shoulders. "We're using a better grade of beef and added two ounces per burger. And the buns are homemade. We add cornmeal, that's the secret."

"Cornmeal." Gus knew what the buns were made of? "You're actually into the restaurant thing, aren't you?"

"I give a hundred percent to every project I take on, Lilah. But what I'm most 'into' is establishing myself in this town. Rebuilding it. It's been dying a slow death for decades. I'm going to put it on the map. Increase job opportunities. Give people driving through a reason to stop. Give young people who leave a reason to come back."

Lilah's eyebrows raised a bit more with each goal he listed. "You do like a challenge. So back to my question. I said you couldn't wait to get out of here when you were younger, and you said that you couldn't stand staying and that it's not the same thing. What do you mean? How is it not the same?"

"When I left, I wasn't running toward something. I was running away from everything I hated."

"You hated Kalamoose."

"I hated the way I *felt* in Kalamoose. It took a long time to realize I'd have felt the same anywhere. I was running from what I was. Leaving here wasn't the answer."

"Coming back is?"

Before he answered, he tapped a finger on the rim of her plate to remind her to eat.

"Coming back is my way of owning the past. Owning my present."

"Not to mention half the town," she quipped, then immediately felt herself turn bright red.

Gus surprised her by laughing—big, free, hearty laughter that said he had no guilt about his current circumstances.

"I've worked hard for everything. I never took my finals in high school, so I got my GED while I was still in prison. When I got out, I worked two jobs so I could go to college and get my business degree. One of my employers became a mentor, like Harm had been. This time I stepped up to the plate, made sure I didn't screw up and found myself working as a financial advisor for people with a lot more money than I ever thought I'd make."

"Did you enjoy it?"

"Enough. What I really enjoyed was learning and eventually investing for myself. I saved money, made good decisions. Met other people who have faith in my visions. And here I am."

She hadn't expected this of him, and it embarrassed her now to realize it. She should have been one of the people who'd had the most faith.

Lilah wasn't sure what surprised her more at the moment—that he'd reached this point in his life or that he was talking to her about it so cordially.

He nodded toward her milk shake.

"Are you going to make a dent in that?"

She assessed the large drink and all the food. "I don't think so."

Unfolding his tall frame, he rose from the booth, stepped to the counter and called to one of the waitresses. "Jill, would you hand me a glass, please?"

Mission accomplished, he returned to the table and poured part of her milk shake into his tumbler. He took a sip, licked the creamy chocolate mustache from his lips and said, "This is one item we're going to keep on the menu."

Lilah tried—and failed miserably—not to stare. She remembered now how much he'd enjoyed milk shakes as a teenager and how much she'd enjoyed watching him drink them. They'd been an occasional treat when he'd saved enough money from his after-school job at the jail to take her into Minot for a meal.

She still recalled the way he'd tipped his head back and how the muscles had moved in his neck as he'd swallowed. He'd make eye contact with her and lick the ice cream off his lip, and she'd scoot closer to him in the booth to kiss away whatever was left....

Quickly lowering her head, she took a huge bite of burger and concentrated on chewing.

"I know what you're thinking."

Endeavoring not to choke, she glanced up.

Gus's eyes shone with awareness. "You're thinking there's a greedy satisfaction to owning a business I could barely afford to patronize in my youth. And there is a lot of satisfaction."

He made the confession with no trouble at all. She nodded and smiled around the bite of burger she hadn't managed to force down yet. "Uh-huh, that's what I'm thinking."

"There are a lot of Lakota in this area. They're still an economically impoverished group. I intend to make them a vital part of the workforce in Kalamoose."

Taking a sip of her shake to wash down the burger, she asked, "By employing most of them yourself?"

He actually grinned. "I'll be creating a lot of jobs with the new business."

"And then you can help people invest their money?"

"I'm good at it."

"Obviously." Laughing, she quipped, "What can you do with a thousand bucks and change?"

"I hope that was a joke." Gus kept his voice low, his eyes narrowed. "You should have a savings at your age. Property, if at all possible. Even if the funds aren't liquid, they should be available without egregious penalty should an emergency arise—"

"Whoa. Hey, I was kidding…exaggerating." A little. She had thirteen hundred bucks now that she was working again.

Obviously she was grievously behind her peers in terms of savings. *So much for the summer home.* She made a mental note to take Bree's savings to a financial advisor as soon as they got back to L.A.

"So. 'Egregious penalties,' huh?" She nodded broadly to lighten the moment. "You must have taken a few English courses in college, too."

Gus didn't look sheepish over his minilecture, but he did relax a bit. "Artistic people aren't always the best future planners."

You're tellin' me. Changing the subject, she asked, "So what made you become a foster parent?"

That was really what she wanted to talk about anyway. Gus, the father.

He had never talked to her about wanting children, hadn't liked other kids even when he was one. Because he had no fondness for his own childhood, Lilah had assumed he'd opt out of raising children.

"There are a lot of Native American kids throughout North and South Dakota who need foster care," he told her. "The preference is to place them with someone who's a tribe member or close to the tribes so their racial heritage can remain intact." He shrugged. "There's a need. I'm helping to fill it."

"That doesn't answer my question. No one raises kids, because, hey, someone's gotta do it." Lord knew she struggled with Bree, with her own doubts and enormous concerns every day. She couldn't imagine anyone choosing parenthood as a philosophical mission.

"The decision to become a parent—a single parent— isn't as easy as deciding to fill a void," she argued. "Especially for someone like you."

Gus's jaw tightened perceptibly, but he didn't argue.

"I didn't mean that in a—"

He raised a hand, halting the qualifier. "Don't apologize for the truth. My father left when I was two, my mother and her family drank alcohol like water. I shouldn't know the first thing about being a father."

"But you do?"

He picked up a paper napkin, wiped his mouth, set the napkin down again and folded its edge. Pausing. Thinking.

"I've had a number of mentors in my life." He looked into Lilah's eyes. "Your uncle was the first. I've learned how to treat people over the years. The biggest regret of my life is that I didn't wise up in time to thank Harm Owens for saving my ass. More than once. But at least I can give someone else a reason to choose the right path. And, now both Elan and I have somewhere we should be for the holidays."

Now he had family that actually felt like family. Lilah saw the mingled pain and satisfaction in his eyes and felt an overwhelming urge to reach across the table to take his hand.

She wished she could say something reassuring or wise about Harm, but the truth was her uncle *had* felt betrayed by Gus's clandestine relationship with her. And he had been bitterly disappointed by Gus's slide into trouble.

After Gus went to prison, Harm had gone to see him, at her request. Gus had refused the meeting and a prison official had said he was often uncooperative. Uncle Harm had wanted her and Gus to go their own ways.

He'd thought it best. And the best way to facilitate a permanent break between them was to allow his own contact with Gus to slip away.

Lilah was sorry for all of them. They'd all made mistakes.

The truth, she knew now, was that everyone was fallible. She hadn't cornered the market on character defects. Even the best of humans could make mistakes that kept on hurting. It was a paradoxically comforting thought. For so long she'd been dividing the world into two camps—the people whose mistakes weren't *so* awful…and her.

"Parenthood scares me," she blurted, and it felt good just to admit that out loud. "I mean, the thought of parenthood. I think it's brave of you to be a foster parent."

"I started out by mentoring. It's a less terrifying way to wade in." He offered a commiserating smile. Tossing aside the napkin he'd been futzing with, he quirked an eyebrow at her. "So who's the girl? From what I remember, she looks just like your sister Sara at that age."

The few bites of hamburger Lilah had taken turned leaden in her stomach. She knew she wasn't ready to share every fact about Bree, and she didn't want to lie outright, so she took a breath and tried to step around potential mines.

"Her name is Sabrina. Bree. Her mother was a good friend of mine. Grace passed away two months ago." Toying with the straw in her shake, she murmured,

"Grace was ill a long time, so she made plans for Bree to stay with me…you know, in the event she didn't pull through. Now we're trying to figure out the next step."

"Are you the girl's legal guardian?"

"Something like that." Looking away, she felt her tired spirits droop. Life was a complicated business. Deciding she didn't want to answer any more questions about Bree, she asked, "How long has your foster son been with you?"

"Six months. How long—"

"And you're definitely going to adopt him?"

"He's legally free to be adopted, so, yes, we'll start that process early next year. We're waiting until Karen—"

The mention of his fiancée made them both pause— Gus in the middle of his sentence, and Lilah with her milk shake halfway to her mouth.

"Karen and I will be adopting Elan together." Gus finished the sentence—more forcefully than necessary.

Lilah nodded and smiled—more heartily than necessary. "That's great." Setting the shake on the table, she looked at her watch. "Oh, wow! I need to go. The bookmobile leaves in a few minutes."

"You need a book?"

"Bree is there. I have to go get her." She slid to the edge of the booth.

"We used to run anywhere wc wanted until it was dark out."

"Those were the days."

Gus rose as she did, and they stood awkwardly for

several long seconds until he held out his hand. "Thanks for coming today, Lilah. I'm glad for the chance to talk more...civilly."

Setting the tone for goodbye with polite formality was definitely a good thing. If only he wasn't holding out his hand. She couldn't reasonably ignore it.

Reaching out for a handshake, Lilah hoped exuberance would cancel out any subtler sensations. She still remembered the very first time she'd held hands with Gus and how shockingly right it had felt. His big, square, warm palm...the fingers that curled gently but possessively around hers....

It still happened. After all these years, his palm still ignited when it connected with hers, sending warmth all the way up her arm. Into her heart. The innocent touch still tingled.

Lilah felt her face heat and looked up to see if the contact affected him as well, but his expression didn't change. It remained polite, a tad formal. As if she was an acquaintance, nothing more. She knew her expression shouldn't change, either, so she kept the too-wide smile in place until her cheeks hurt.

"Thanks so much for lunch."

He wisely refrained from mentioning that she'd barely touched it.

She began to sidle past him, having trouble breaking eye contact while she sidestepped toward the diner's entrance.

Gus watched her, turning as required to keep her in

sight. She walked without seeing anything but him until she heard Gloria bark, "Behind you!" The aging waitress had a row of hot plates balanced on her bare forearm. Lilah muttered a hasty apology, aligned her gaze and her feet toward the door and left without looking back again.

As she jammed a key in her car's ignition, she hoped the shaky feeling inside was due to low blood sugar and not to a scary, scary yearning to spend more time with another woman's fiancé.

Shoving the stick shift into Reverse, she pulled away from the diner. She'd had no right to come here today, full of ire and pain and righteous indignation over the fact that he might have cheated on her. Their relationship had been over for more than a decade. Nothing he'd done when they were kids fell under the heading "Lilah's Business" today.

Yanking the shift into Drive, she took a last, reluctant look at the diner in her rearview mirror, then hit the gas and pulled out of the parking lot, hoping the scrunch of tires on gravel would drown the rapid, loud beat of her heart.

Within a couple hundred feet of the diner her body began to tremble in earnest. So much so that she pulled to the side of the road, hands clutching the wheel, eyes closed as she tried to calm herself.

By the time she'd turned seventeen, she'd known unequivocally what she would do with her future. Even as her relationship with Gus progressed, her plans remained the same: graduate high school and use the money she earned from her summer jobs to move to Hollywood. Committed to pursuing her dream, she'd simply taken for granted that he would move with her. Then Gus was arrested, and ditching him became unthinkable. Although he wouldn't see her, wouldn't even talk to her, helping him became all she thought about. She'd have shouted news of their relationship from the top of the Savings and Loan if it would have helped the situation. She settled for confessing to Uncle Harm, trying not to shrink beneath the sad, knowing look in his eyes as she asked for his help. But Gus no longer wanted assistance from her or Harm or anyone else in Kalamoose.

After graduation, Lilah went to work for Ernie, serving tables and washing dishes at the diner, telling herself she was working for both their futures, certain he'd be out of jail soon and would eventually forgive her. They would leave Kalamoose together.

The reality didn't come close to her plan.

Gus went from jail to prison.

And she turned from a seventeen-year-old girl with boyfriend problems into a young woman with a much bigger issue to face.

Before Gus forgave her, before his case even went to court, and long, long before she felt ready to deal with life's greatest responsibility, Lilah discovered she was pregnant. Terrified, she told only one person. Together she and Harm made a plan—for the baby, for Lilah, and without his knowing, even for Gus. For once in her life, Lilah followed Harm's advice to the letter.

Forehead resting against the steering wheel, Lilah wished Uncle Harm were here now. She wished there was at least one other person she could talk to who knew the truth, because she felt almost as confused and frightened and isolated today as she had at seventeen. The trouble with secrets was that one tended to give birth to another. Now she felt like a spider caught in a web much bigger than she'd intended to build, and the threads were beginning to tear under strain.

Run, a voice whispered, and oh, it was tempting. But worse than the anger and resentment the truth would surely stir, Lilah feared that if she ran again, she might never find her way home.

Chapter Ten

When Sara came home from work that night, Bree was in her room reading the fourth Harry Potter, which she'd borrowed from the bookmobile, and Lilah was cleaning the kitchen after dinner—chicken à la gunpowder. She'd been attempting to prepare homemade meals for Bree, an experiment in creation that so far made Frankenstein's monster look like a success story.

She read the recipes; she bought all the right ingredients. She didn't know what kept going wrong. Last night's Swedish meatballs had resembled good old North Dakota hockey pucks. Tonight's culinary adventure was supposed to have been a Mexican-influenced poultry dish. Well, she must have used the wrong kind of peppers or mismeasured some ingredient, because after one bite she and Bree had both hightailed it for the faucet to douse the flames in their mouths.

Bree had returned to the table with an expression bordering on panic.

"Do I have to taste the potatoes?" she'd asked, and Lilah had felt sure that a social worker would knock on the door at any minute.

As bonding experiences went, tonight had not been a good one.

Morose, Lilah screwed the lid back on the peanut butter jar and made a mental note to buy more. Poor Bree wasn't even complaining about all the PB&J's she'd eaten this week; she just went to the fridge herself and slapped the nut butter on the bread after another failed dinner.

Tears filled Lilah's eyes.

At seventeen she had made an adoption plan for her child, because she'd known she wasn't capable of being a good mother. She'd hoped time had blessed her with more adequate skills.

It didn't look that way.

Jamming a plug in the drain, she turned on the faucet and set her hands and mind to washing dishes, but the time she'd spent with Gus today brought so many emotions to life. All afternoon a logjam of tears had clogged her throat.

Lilah felt no relief when Sara entered the house through the kitchen door. Rinsing jam off a plastic plate, she grumbled, "You're late. Dinner is over." As if there had been any dinner to give her.

"That's okay, I grabbed something out."

Irrationally, Lilah slapped her sponge on the counter. "But you knew I was going to try a new meal tonight!"

Crossing to the refrigerator before she even removed her gun belt, Sara withdrew a half-gallon jug of chocolate milk and swigged straight from the container. "Did it work?" she asked when she came up for air.

Lilah hurled the sponge into the sink. "It was fabulous!" With a vicious twist she shut the faucet.

Sara raised an auburn brow. "Good. 'Cause I've got something to tell you, and it has to do with food." Ignoring Lilah's crossed arms and obvious frustration, she said, "I got a job for you here in town. Food service."

Reaching to the top of the refrigerator, Sara fished around in a woven basket and came away with a handful of mini foil-covered peanut-butter cups. Unwrapping one, she popped it into her mouth. "You start tomorrow."

Lilah squinted. "I start what tomorrow? I already looked into jobs in Kalamoose." She flapped a hand. "There weren't any."

"This one just came up." Sara shucked the wrapper onto the counter, opened another chocolate and added it to her calorie allotment for the day. "Fortunately for you, I was in the right place at the right time. I had dinner at the diner and found out Gloria doesn't want to work nights anymore. She said they're looking for someone to replace her. *Someone with experience.*

Sooo, I told her you served celebrities in L.A. and if they could trust you not to spill soup on Tom Cruise in Hollywood, they could sure as hell trust you at Ernie's. And you worked there before, so you know the diner." She rolled the foil into a tiny ball, tossed it into the sink from over her shoulder and grinned, appearing absolutely certain and inordinately pleased that she had solved her sister's dilemma.

Lilah spoke the first words that entered her mind. "I can't work at Ernie's Diner!"

Sara stopped grinning. "Why the hell not?"

"Because. I'm not going to be hired there, for one." Watching her sister closely, Lilah said, "You must know who the new owner is."

"'Course I do! That ought to make it a sure bet. The way I see it, he owes us one after landing himself in prison. Made Uncle Harm look like a fool for believing in him."

"Well, he doesn't owe me anything."

"I thought you helped him become a snappy dresser."

Lilah said nothing for a moment. She saw no sign that Sara had any idea about her and Gus.

In some ways that was a disappointment: shouldn't sisters know the most important parts of each other's lives? Shouldn't they be each other's confidantes and sounding boards?

Lilah knew as little about Sara's love life as Sara knew about hers. Did Sara even have a love life? Though Lilah harbored a private suspicion that her sister had been nursing a crush on their neighbor Nick since Sara was in pigtails, the two of them seemed to genuinely dislike each other. Whenever Lilah and Nettie had questioned their big sis about men, Sara had merely grumbled that they were more trouble than they were worth and then closed the discussion.

"You went off to college before I started my sophomore year in high school. I got to know Gus a little better around then," Lilah ventured, looking for any indication at all that Sara knew about their romance.

Sara's thin auburn eyebrows drew together, making her appear impatient. "Yeah? And?"

Quickly Lilah decided Sara was still in the dark and decided to leave her there, for the moment at any rate.

"He and I didn't leave school on very good terms."

"Well, duh. From what I heard when I came home the summer after you graduated, no one was on very good terms with him. He was a troublemaker." She turned around to root through a cabinet stuffed with snack goods. "He looks like he's straightened up some. Hasn't caused any problems since he's been back, except when he first bought Ernie's. That caused a ruckus, I can tell you, until word got around that he was leaving the chicken-fried steak platter on the menu."

Pulling a handful of cookies from a package of Nutter Butters, she pointed a peanut-shaped cookie at Lilah. "I'd think you'd be willing to deal with him just so you could work closer to home. You've got that kid to think of."

"Stop calling her 'that kid.'"

"She doesn't mind."

That was true. So far, Bree was getting along fine with Sara; they had the same taste in food.

"Minot's a long way to go for a graveyard shift," Sara persisted. "I can't guarantee I'll always be here at night. What if I get a call?"

"How often does that happen in Kalamoose?" Lilah tried to laugh the question off, but she knew there were plenty of other reasons to stick closer to home and keep tabs on Bree.

Sara chewed her cookie angrily before speaking. "Why does everyone think we're crime-free? There's a hotbed of activity all over this area. The Gentleman Caller is still on the loose, you know."

"Are you still harping on that guy?" For two years Sara had been devoted to the idea that of all the law enforcers in North Dakota, she would be the one to nab the infamous Gentleman Caller, a bank robber whose good manners made him a state celebrity. Sara had even arrested Nettie's husband—before they'd married, thankfully—convinced that Chase was the suave thief.

"Isn't there some governing body of sheriffs that's going to get upset if you arrest any more innocent men?"

Lilah meant the remark to be teasing, but she realized her mistake immediately when a fine spray of cookie crumbs dusted the floor as Sara choked.

"Real damned funny!" her sister growled. She grabbed the package of Nutter Butters, the thin plastic container crackling noisily in her punishing hands, and stomped from the kitchen.

"Sara!" Lilah started after her. "Come back. I didn't mean—" The kitchen door swung shut in her face.

Lilah exhaled heavily and gave up the chase. It was better to let Sara blow off steam before trying to talk to her, even to apologize, once she was in a rage. Dejectedly, Lilah returned to the sink to wipe it down and wring out the sponge.

Another night shot to hell.

Evening after evening for the past two weeks, the story was the same: she cleaned the kitchen after an unsatisfactory dinner and then tried to rest before work, while Bree holed up in her room with a book and Sara surfed the Internet for information on America's most wanted criminals.

Maybe she ought to apply for the job at the diner; at least it would give her something to do earlier in the evening.

As soon as she pictured it, she shook her head.

Even if Gus hired her, to see him every day would be…

She shuddered. Nope. Couldn't even go there. Too awkward, too many unresolved feelings. Too many times she would look in his eyes and remember his lips.

Stuffing the sponge in its suction-cup holder, she pushed through the swinging door and tromped upstairs to try to nap before she made the late-night trek into Minot. Usually she knocked on Bree's room and received a curt admonishment that kids ought to be left to read in peace since it was good for them.

As Lilah didn't particularly feel like being rebuffed

again tonight, she headed for her old room, lay down on the bed and stared at an ancient crack in the pale-pink ceiling. So many plans made in this pretty, girl's room. So many dreams.

As drowsiness overtook her, she wondered what Bree daydreamed about and hoped that someday she would know.

Then, as her eyes closed, she pictured Gus and his pride as he told her about his business, about Elan... about the dreams he was living without her. In the last seconds before sleep, she had the courage to whisper, "Good for you, my love."

Heat and coffee. Gus felt the first, smelled the latter as a steaming mug tickled his nose like smelling salts.

"Rise and shine." A sweet voice wakened him further.

Lifting his head from the back of the couch, Gus winced and rubbed his aching neck. When his gaze focused on a slim brunette offering the coffee and a brief, understanding squeeze of his shoulder, he realized with a stab of guilt that he'd fallen asleep. Again.

Accepting the caffeine, he offered a sincerely apologetic smile. "How long was I out this time?"

His fiancée shrugged. "About forty minutes. It's almost ten o'clock."

Ten o'clock. In the evening. They'd been talking about the theory of multiple intelligences, he'd yawned and Karen had jumped up to make coffee. Must have had to reheat it a few times by now.

Gus shook his head, wiping a hand down his face. "I'm sorry."

He had arrived in Chicago that morning with just enough time to get to his first meeting, a schmooze over overpriced pastry to convince three prominent Chicago businesspeople, Karen's father among them, to invest in his dream of a year-round educational/vocational center for young adults who'd fallen through the cracks of mainstream institutions.

He'd spent the rest of the day in more meetings, this time regarding his own investments, then headed to Karen's where he'd fallen asleep on her sofa. He was rotten company. Worse, he'd been in Chicago twelve hours and hadn't stopped thinking about Lilah for five minutes, except when he was dozing.

"I like your plans for pod-style work spaces, by the way," Karen said, equably ignoring the fact that her fiancé had been moody and distracted from the moment he'd said hello. "Experience shows they work very well in classrooms." She seated herself one sofa cushion away from him and sipped her coffee.

Gus murmured something agreeable in return. They'd been apart for weeks and so far had discussed only pleasantries, no mention of the wedding date they needed to set or anything else personal.

He blamed himself.

Making a more concerted effort, he asked about her summer school class at Chicago Village School. Unfortunately, during an animated description of a kid named

Dakota, who had a penchant for sticking pennies in apples and feeding them to the guinea pig, his mind wandered.

He'd been hoping—hard—that coming here tonight would cure the disquiet in his heart. Lilah was a young boy's dream; Karen was the right woman for the man he'd become. He was about to adopt Elan and wanted more kids eventually. Logic said his future was in this room.

He focused on his fiancée, searched for an appropriate response to the guinea pig story, but noticed something else.

"Where's your ring?"

Baffled at first by the abrupt question, she glanced at her bare ring finger. And flushed.

"Oh! It was clay day at school. We're making handprints the children can paint. You know how messy clay is, and…the ring has so many little diamonds." Sighing, she laughed at herself. "I'm always afraid I'm going to ruin it or lose it. I still need to get it sized."

Gus had surprised her two months ago with a large, perfectly cut diamond in an elaborate antique-style setting. He'd had to guess at the size, but certainly expected her to have had it adjusted by now. Karen alphabetized her CDs. She did her own taxes. She was one of the most efficient people he'd ever known. For some reason, the fact that her engagement ring still didn't fit disturbed him.

"If the ring doesn't suit you, we can get another," he said, hearing annoyance instead of generosity in his tone.

Startled, she shook her head. "No, it's fine. It's…a handsome ring."

"Karen, it's not fine if it isn't right for you." He tried to remember her expression when he proposed. Had she liked the ring then? The details were fuzzy. "Have you seen a style you like better?"

"No."

"Maybe one with a different kind of stone," he suggested.

"It's not necessary."

But Gus felt it was necessary. Something was clearly wrong; the options were ignore it or fix it. If it could be fixed at all.

"We could replace the center stone with a ruby."

"I don't want—"

Karen set her coffee mug on the table, clasped her hands on her lap and looked away. She allowed her usually placid expression to fall into a troubled frown.

Discomfort mounted. It had been so long since Gus had been in love, crazy love, he'd almost convinced himself that what he'd felt for Lilah had been nothing more than a boy's reaction to a gorgeous young girl.

Karen was everything he'd told himself he wanted, a gift for straightening up and flying right. His relationship with her was proof that a man could change, that he could rewrite his past. From the very beginning their relationship had been steady and peaceful. He'd been selfish.

"I'm not a good fiancé, am I?" When her cheeks reddened again, he knew it was true. He'd thought a meeting of minds, shared values could stand in for true passion. He knew himself well enough to know he would never cheat on her and had told himself he would give her every good thing in life.

Like a ring that didn't fit.

"It's not nearly enough, is it?"

Surprise flashed across Karen's face. Then something shifted. Her surprise turned to sadness, and she reached over to squeeze his hand.

Even as Gus prepared to do the right thing, to have a conversation that was composed, understanding, direct, he knew he would walk away the loser in this scenario. She would move on, to a man worthy of her gentle, calm brand of love. And he…

He shook his head, the irony of his life apparent to him. No matter how far he'd traveled, he'd always been headed home. The respectable man he'd become still struggled with the boy he'd been, and the boy was destined to love in a way that was wild and fierce, or not at all.

Ding, ding, ding. "Order up!"

With a voice as burly as his shoulders, Carl "Cookie" McCoy slid two meat loaf specials into the service window at Minot's Pie 'n' Burger restaurant.

Lilah, the only waitress on duty at 1:00 a.m., paused in her mission of filling jam pots for tomorrow's breakfast shift, wiped her sticky fingers on a bleach-soaked bar towel and reached for the hot plates.

The scent of diluted bleach mingled with the aromas of meat loaf, mashed potatoes, brown gravy and canned peas. *Ugh.*

Cookie grinned as she reached into the window. A gold crown winked at her. "You want to get breakfast when your shift is over? I know a place with great hash."

Lilah refrained from rolling her eyes. Cookie asked her the same question every night, although the lure was always different: great hash, great flapjacks, great java, great spuds. She shook her head. "I'm watching my cholesterol."

"You're gonna say yes one morning."

"No, I'm not," she sang, stepping back with her plates, "because I know there's a Mrs. Cookie, and she'd take me down."

Cookie flapped a big paw at her. "Don't let her stop you from following your heart."

Lilah didn't even bother not to laugh at that. The man was about sixty years old, stood six foot two and weighed two-fifty if he weighed an ounce, which made him only slightly smaller than the wife he routinely managed to overlook.

Moving to a new topic, she said, "I need a chili omelette with extra onions and cheese for table five."

He grumbled something as she turned away then called after her, "Don't forget to hang your ticket, Miss By-The-Book."

Lilah balanced the meat loaf plates on one arm, grabbed two huge white dinner rolls with the other hand

and headed to her table, where a couple of hungry truckers had heard her exchange with the cook.

She nearly cringed at the looks in their eyes. *Oh, please give me a break and do not make me a "better" offer.*

Avoiding eye contact, she slid their meals in front of them, took note of their coffee cups, which she was sorry to see she was going to have to refill, and said, "Are you all set?"

"So you don't like hash. How do you feel about French toast?"

Dear God. Her prospective paramour was younger than Cookie by a few years and possessed a tattooed I-know-what-a-lady-likes charisma he had no doubt plied on beleaguered waitresses up and down the interstate.

Too tired to quip, she murmured, "Can't. I'm allergic to eggs."

He raised an unruly eyebrow. "French fries? French…anything?"

"I'm engaged. To a Scotsman. You know how they feel about the French."

Both men looked confused. "No."

Neither did she, but what the hell? "Enjoy your meal."

Reaching into the pocket of her apron as she left the table, she closed her fingers around the modest wad of cash and bigger collection of coins she'd earned since midnight.

I am doing this for Bree, she reminded herself. *Children need three meals a day.* Plus snacks, and Cookie let her take home the two-day-old cinnamon rolls.

She yawned as she headed for the coffeepot then realized that another booth had been occupied.

The need for more tips warred with her desire to hide in the walk-in freezer for the rest of her shift. *Please don't let it be another jerky guy who thinks a waitress is an easy mark.*

Peeking around the coffeemaker, she had to blink her eyes, look away then look again before she could positively I.D. the man who had obeyed the Seat Yourself sign.

Ensconced in the booth, his arms resting on the tabletop, Gus looked anything but delighted by his surroundings. His shoulders were tight, expression grim and sculpted jaw clenched as he gazed steadily in her direction.

Obviously this wasn't a coincidence.

Lilah felt a jolt of energy that may have signaled excitement or quite possibly an incipient panic attack. Automatically she smoothed her apron over the denims she was allowed to wear and wished she'd opted for more than mascara on her lashes and a claw clip in her hair.

Making eye contact, she offered a brief nod of acknowledgment, which Gus returned just as briefly.

"Be right with you," she said, then took time to collect herself by putting up a new pot of coffee. When she was breathing steadily, she quite deliberately removed the book of checks and pencil from her apron pocket and approached Gus's table.

"Hi. Welcome to Pie 'n' Burger. What can I get you?"

Gus half smiled. "What do you suggest at—" he checked his watch "—one-thirty in the morning?"

"I'd suggest putting your pillow over your head and going back to bed. But apparently you passed on that option. Are you hungry?"

"What do you have that's sweet?"

Lilah narrowed her eyes then remembered this was Gus, not Dumb and Dumber from the table on the other side of the room. He wasn't flirting.

"The cinnamon rolls are good. We put butter and icing on before we nuke them and then more butter on top. Guaranteed to clog a major artery in fifteen minutes or your money back."

"With a sales pitch like that, how can I resist? A cinnamon roll and coffee."

"Decaf?"

Gus shook his head. "I'm catching a red-eye to New York. I may as well stay up."

"You're going to the airport? That's what you're doing in Minot?"

He eyed her speculatively. "That's what I'll be doing in Minot at five a.m. At one-thirty I'm here to talk to you."

It wasn't good that his words sent a quiver of anticipation through her stomach. Just like old times.

"What do you want to talk about?"

Gus leaned back in his chair. "Do you have a couple of minutes?"

"I need to refill coffees and check on the progress of a chili omelette."

"All right." He cocked his head at her, considering. "I'll wait."

Tonight he was exactly the Gus she remembered— the sexy, dark bad boy with thoughts she couldn't read.

"I'll get your coffee." Lilah turned, interested in more than the size of her tips for the first time since she'd come to work here.

Behind the counter, she took the spatula they used to butter and ice the cinnamon rolls and put the usual slab on top of the sweet bun, then removed half as an after-thought. A stranger's arteries were one thing; she didn't want to kill Gus before he had a chance to tell her why he was here.

Glancing toward Cookie, who insisted, "It's the butter that brings 'em back," she slid the dish into the microwave and pressed the buttons.

Grabbing the fresh pot of coffee, she headed into the dining room again. Without looking in Gus's direction she knew he was watching her. As nonchalantly as she could, she filled the other diners' cups first, including a stop at the truckers' table to give them an extra dose of caffeine.

"How is everything?" she asked perfunctorily.

When neither man answered immediately, she met their eyes. And was sorry.

The trucker who'd come on to her the first time kept his head lowered toward his meat loaf, but the other fellow now took it upon himself to pick up where his friend had left off.

"I wouldn't set my alarm clock just to eat hash with

that guy, either," he said, hitching his chin toward his friend. He put a hand on her wrist as she tried to pour the coffee. "I'm Dodge. And you're—" he read her name tag "—Lilah. Sexy name for a sexy dame."

Oh, barf.

With the nearly full coffeepot in her hand, the pressure he put on her forearm forced her to lean down. She braced her elbow on the table so she wouldn't drop the pot. Her temper bristled. "That's a very hot pot of coffee, Dodge. I wouldn't want to drop it."

"The coffee ain't the only thing that's hot around here." Dodge, who appeared to be roughly the same age and bulk as his friend, but sported more tattoos, dropped his gaze to her chest. When his eyes met hers again, he looked alarmingly serious. "Why don't you put the pot down? Sit a minute." He kept his hand right where it was. "Don't you want to hear *my* plans for breakfast?"

Had bumping around in a truck all day unhinged his brain? Had that come-on *ever* worked for him?

Lilah had begun her restaurant career in dives just like this one. She'd made a point of working in more upscale establishments for the last several years, but she remembered her earlier training. She'd learned how to handle guys like Dodge from waitresses who had spent too many years putting up with this kind of crap.

"I'm going to need my hand back, Dodge. I'm working."

"I can think of better things to do with those pretty

hands than serve coffee." He loosened his hold, but slid beefy fingers up her arm. His voice and his touch were, she assumed, meant to be seductive, but the only goose bumps they aroused were the kind that usually came from watching scary movies.

She might have attempted to extricate herself with words had she not been so tired or so ticked off that her life had come to this: serving greasy food to men who thought they could turn her on by flexing tattoos with other women's names.

I was Kalamoose Chokecherry Princess three years running, butthead.

Offering her best beauty queen smile—big and pretty and as genuine as a three-dollar bill—she drew the coffeepot away, just enough to line it up with the tall tumbler of ice water to the right of Dodge's plate. Then she pulled the pot back like a bat and swung, connecting with the plastic tumbler and sending it sailing into Dodge's lap.

Home run, she congratulated herself silently as the brawny truck driver took a moment to figure out what had happened to his crotch. Once it sunk in, so to speak, he released an expletive that rang throughout the restaurant.

"You did that on purpose!"

Ya think?

His friend guffawed heartily, obviously thrilled that it hadn't happened to him and that his companion hadn't had any more luck than he.

Before Lilah could embark on the profuse, if insincere, apology, which was stage two of the that-ain't-no-way-to-treat-a-waitress lesson plan, a body positioned itself between her and Dodge. The trucker was rising from his now wet seat, and he did not look like he wanted to shake hands and make up.

Gus's suited shoulder did double duty as it blocked her from Dodge and held Lilah back. Not that she intended to tangle any further; the truck driver was taller than she'd thought and she was beginning to entertain the notion that words would have worked better than ice water, after all.

"Now that was a damn shame," Gus said, managing to sound confused as to how the water had been spilled. "I've told Lulu a million times she's not cut out for food service."

Dodge looked bewildered, as if he'd expected a fight and wasn't sure whether or not Gus was starting or avoiding one. "I thought her name was Lilah," he said suspiciously.

Gus shook his head. "That's her stage name. She wants to go to Hollywood and be a star. Left me and our five little ones to pursue the dream, but I'm here to convince her to come home. Waiting tables isn't for her. She's very clumsy."

"*Five* little ones?" Dodge looked as if he needed to shake water from his ear.

"The youngest is only three months."

"Not even weaned?" Appalled, Dodge gaped.

Gus shrugged. "Not of his own free will."

The big man shook his head in patent disapproval.

He glared over Gus's shoulder. "A woman shouldn't run out on her kids. And formula ain't good for babies. My wife says it screws with their immunization systems. She's a dedicated mother."

"And I bet you show her your appreciation every chance you get," Gus said.

"Damned right." Dodge, the two-faced cheat, completely missed the irony. Lilah slipped farther behind Gus's back so she could roll her eyes.

"Maybe if you showed more of *your* appreciation—" he pointed one sausagelike finger at Gus "—she'd stay put where she belongs. I can tell you she's gonna go broke as a waitress."

Gus nodded. "I hear you." Stepping aside, he grabbed Lilah's arm. The grip, she thought, was a little tighter than strictly necessary.

She attempted to tug away, but decided not to argue when he held on and growled out of the side of his mouth, "Come on, Lu."

Chapter Eleven

Pulling her toward his table, he asked in a low voice, "Is there anyone else on this shift with you?"

"No." Lilah felt amused, but mildly discombobulated, as well. "That was very weird," she said as they reached his table. "Since when do you make up stories for people?"

"Since I got out of prison and decided I didn't want to go back in. Do you always handle disputes that way?"

"When the dispute is with a Neanderthal trucker with wandering hands and eyes, yeah, I do."

They arrived at the table, and he let go of her arm.

"Thanks for the rescue," she said, smiling, but Gus didn't look much like an angel avenging her honor.

"I wasn't rescuing you," he said—rather unheroically, she thought. "I was protecting my interests. I came here to talk, and I'm losing sleep to do it."

Lilah crossed her arms, irritated by his sudden chilliness. "Fine. So talk."

Ding, ding, ding. "Order up!" Cookie called from the service window.

Lilah looked at Gus. He sighed. "Try not to throw water on anyone else." She turned away. "And hurry."

As Lilah picked up the omelet she'd ordered for table five and the cinnamon roll she'd nuked for Gus, Cookie poked his balding head out from the kitchen. "What the hell happened on table eight?"

"I had a little accident."

"That's not what it sounded like. Take a towel out. He's still trying to mop up his seat. And why didn't you tell me you was married with five kids when you interviewed?"

"Why didn't I what— Oh."

After a glance at the table where Gus had once again taken his seat, Cookie narrowed his eyes at Lilah. "You and me are havin' a talk after your shift. Plan on it."

Lilah had to get back to Bree right after work, and she had a subzero desire to drag this particular shift on any longer than necessary. Giving Cookie a half smile while she brainstormed ways to get out of the talk, she grabbed what she needed and headed to her tables, hoping he would forget about her once the breakfast crew came on.

After delivering the omelet and wiping the remaining moisture from Dodge's booth, she placed Gus's cinnamon roll in front of him and dropped his ticket on the table.

"I can't sit down. My boss is getting touchy. He thinks you're my husband and that you're here to talk instead of eat."

"Then he shouldn't mind if you sit down so we can repair our relationship and save the family...Lulu."

His smile said his words were meant to be wry, but Lilah felt a little jolt of discomfort.

"I'll stand," she murmured. "I still need this job."

"What I have to say will hopefully make this job a moot point." He pulled the cinnamon roll toward him and poised his fork over the melting butter and icing. "This looks like a heart attack waiting to happen. Is the taste worth it?"

"Depends on how dangerously you like to live. I already heard that Gloria is leaving the diner," she said, saving him the trouble of telling her. "I don't want to wait tables in Kalamoose."

His eyebrows rose in surprise. "Seems like a fine alternative to waiting tables fifty miles from home at two in the morning."

"Easy for you to say. You moved home and bought half the city. I drove up in a car that's so old the last mechanic I went to asked if it was an antique."

"Ah. It's a pride thing."

"Yeah, it's a pride thing," she agreed, because that was soooo much easier than telling him she didn't want to see him every day. "And I can't believe you're even asking me to work for you. What happened to 'let's stay away from each other'?"

"That's still the best course. But circumstance necessitates a change of heart, and I've learned not to allow my moods to dictate my actions. 'Pride goeth before a fall,' or hadn't you heard?"

"I heard. But when you've fallen as far I have, what's another few feet? Anyway, I'm curious," she persisted. "Why ask me? There have got to be other people who want the job."

"I'm sure there are," he agreed, "and I fully intend to hire one of them." Taking a bite of the cinnamon roll, he chewed and frowned, pushing the dish away. "You should have dinner sometime at Northern Lights. There are dishes there that are worth the cholesterol."

"I'll put that on my to-do list." She whisked the cinnamon roll off the table. "What do you mean you fully intend to hire someone else? Why are you here then? And cut to the chase, because I have tips to make."

"With your unparalleled graciousness and the ability to soak your patrons at ten paces, I'm sure you'll do beautifully." He took a sip of coffee, winced—for effect, she was sure, because the coffee at Pie 'n' Burger wasn't half-bad when she made it—and said, "I'm not here to offer you Gloria's position. I've organized a summer camp that will run for six weeks on my property. I need a drama coach, and you, Ms. Owens, appear to be the only game in town."

Surprise threw her off her game. It took a moment to recoup before she said, "Wow. *Wow.* That is just...oh, my goodness...the most flattering offer I've had in ages!"

"Really?"

"*No!* I 'appear to be the only game in town'? Do you realize you sound desperate?"

"We are. Clea Scolari, the new drama teacher at the high school, agreed to do it, but she's four months pregnant and was just put on bed rest."

"Mmm-hmm. Well, what happened to Mr. Fox, the 'old' drama teacher?"

"Retired to Florida."

"So get someone from Minot."

"I tried. Even sat in on a community theater production of *Annie.* Had a drink with the director afterward. He doesn't like kids."

Suspicion waved a red flag. "When did you see the show and talk to this director?"

Gus pretended to have to think about it. "Few hours ago."

Lilah wanted to lob the cinnamon roll at him. "So you didn't come to Minot to talk to me. You came here after you talked to everybody else."

"Why does that upset you? You don't want the job."

"You approached people who have never worked outside of North Dakota, I bet," she accused. "I am a Hollywood actress. It would have made sense to come to me first."

"You said your career never made it off the ground."

"By *Hollywood* standards. Compared to the people around here, I'm a freaking superstar!"

His expression remained remarkably neutral, almost impassive. "You would like the job then?"

He'd managed to come full circle.

"I didn't say that." She knew she *shouldn't* say that, and narrowed her eyes. "What does the job pay, how long will it last and can Bree be in the program for free?"

Lilah had no idea, of course, whether Bree had any interest whatsoever in attending the summer camp, but if she could attend for free, the job might—just *might*—be a good idea.

"Have you ever taught drama before?" Gus asked in lieu of answering her questions. Realizing that he wasn't going to hand her the job even if she was interested, Lilah felt a twinge of surprise. Her competitive streak kicked in.

"How do you think I supported myself while I established my acting career?"

"By waiting tables."

"Besides that!"

Conveniently ignoring that she had not actually established an acting career and she had never in her life taught a class, drama or any other, Lilah rolled her eyes in exasperation.

Gus watched her speculatively for a moment, then reached into his pocket. Withdrawing his wallet, he pulled out a twenty-dollar bill and laid it on the table. Then he removed a business card and held it up for her examination.

"This has the number to my home office. Call me in two days. I'll be back from New York by then, and we can discuss the details."

Lilah was still holding the coffeepot and the plate with his cinnamon roll. She would have set the plate down to take the card, but his hand reached out. The apron that wrapped around her flat abdomen and hips had two wide pockets. He tucked the card into the pocket closest to him and winked. "Don't forget."

Rising, he prepared to leave.

"Wait a second. I'll get your change."

"Keep it." He lowered his voice. "I think you'll be all right with your trucker friends now, but your boss has been glaring a hole in your back. Maybe you should cut your losses here and leave now."

"And miss the Christmas bonus? No can do. I hear we're getting a canned ham this year."

"Funny. If you work for me, I'll expect you to quit this gig. I have no patience with tardiness for any reason or with employees who perform below expectation because they're too tired to do their jobs."

"Then you'd better answer me next time I ask how much the job pays, hadn't you? I need to get back to my real job now, not stand around chatting with you about a hypothetical one."

His lips curled. "Call me."

After Gus moved his car from the parking lot of the Pie 'n' Burger to a space conveniently across the street, he cut the engine, hunkered down in the seat and watched the coffee shop.

He hadn't lied when he'd said he needed to be at the airport for a flight to New York, though he knew now he was going to miss that flight and would have to wait around and pay for another.

Recalling the trucker's face when Lilah sent the glass of ice water flying toward his crotch, Gus grinned. Big. She knew how to take care of herself, that was for certain. And yet, he felt compelled to make sure there was no ugly backlash to her actions. At the very least, he wanted to watch the truckers leave quietly and not return.

Even though he was confident about her ability to take care of herself physically, he'd always felt protective of her emotional life, even in high school. When she dreamed, she dreamed so big. He remembered being afraid of the fall she could take from such a height.

In high school his dreams had never been as grand as hers. It was only later, fueled by his resentment and by a burning need to make her sorry she'd walked away, that he began to pursue loftier goals. Lilah, he'd discovered, could motivate a man like Helen of Troy. With all the dangerous implications.

He'd lied about going to the play earlier this evening. And, he'd lied about having drinks with the nonexistent play's nonexistent director.

Hooking one wrist over the steering wheel, he lowered his head, rubbed his eyes and swore to himself that helping her would serve as a last act of respect for Harm. Emphasis on *last*. He wouldn't be here at all if her sister Sara hadn't come to Ernie's suggesting—forcefully— that Lilah was in desperate need of a job closer to home.

Sara had further suggested that Gloria's soon-to-be vacated position would do nicely, which was when Gus realized he knew Lilah better than her own family did.

He had no trouble with honest work of any sort, but Lilah didn't belong in a restaurant, serving home fries at one a.m.

He looked toward the shabby coffee shop, where he could see the brightly lit interior through a wall of broad plate-glass windows, and squinted as he caught a glimpse of a high, curling blond ponytail. Lilah Owens was meant for more.

He'd had her on a pedestal so damned long; he might as well keep her there.

When Sara had insisted on Lilah's suitability for Gloria's job, he'd told her there were already a few applicants for the position, but that he would, of course, process Lilah's application as any other should she choose to come in and fill out a form. He was certain she never would.

Thoughts of her had plagued him the rest of the afternoon. Was she in financial distress? Would she be too proud to ask him for a job?

While he'd packed for his business trip to New York, he'd hit on the notion of offering her a job at the summer camp he and Karen had planned.

Karen.

By the time he'd left Chicago, he had an *ex*-fiancée. The more he and Karen had talked, the more he'd realized the ring was, indeed, not the only piece of their engagement that didn't fit. She'd had misgivings about leaving her job, misgivings about living in rural North Dakota, and, clearly, misgivings about the two of them.

He could have reassured her, or at least made the attempt. But his best reasons for wanting to marry Karen became obscured in the blinding light of one fact: he wasn't finished with Lilah. He didn't even know what that meant, really. Not yet. He only knew that Karen deserved more than a man whose attention was back in North Dakota with a woman who drove him half crazy with desire, who could send him to an early grave from sheer anger, and who, more than any other human being, made him feel…connected.

At the end of the night, he and Karen had parted company; she, with notable relief seasoning her regret; he, with a sense of resignation, as if he'd known from the moment he'd first seen Lilah again that they were destined to finish what they'd started as kids. For better or worse.

Accepting that Lilah was, once again, his fate, Gus allowed his muscles to relax. Wishing he'd taken a cup of coffee to go, he settled into the job of protecting the woman who was, ironically, his own greatest danger.

Chapter Twelve

"I'm very grateful for this opportunity, Gus."

Lilah shook her head, not liking the sound of the words. *Too beholden and too serious.* Smiling widely, she tried again.

"This is great! I can't wait to start!"

Yech. Too bubbly.

Consciously relaxing her grip on the steering wheel, she composed her features. "Thanks for the job, Gus. I know we'll work well together."

Looking in the rearview mirror, she gave her reflection an encouraging nod. *That's good. Casual. Upbeat. Grateful, yet confident.*

She tried not to worry about the fact she'd been

talking to herself for the past three days, ever since she'd phoned Gus to tell him she would take the drama coach position. Now she was on her way to the property where he was building his home and planned to hold the camp.

She hadn't seen him for a week.

She knew he'd parked his car outside the restaurant and waited for her shift to end. He'd been asleep in the driver's seat with his head turned toward the coffee shop when she'd emerged from the restaurant. She'd realized immediately that he had been waiting for her, that he was there to make sure she'd be okay after the altercation with the truckers.

She'd been taking care of herself for so many years, packing mace in her purse, right next to the pepper spray, seeing Gus asleep in his car should have made her laugh.

Instead, she'd had bittersweet tears streaming down her cheeks the entire drive home. It had been years since someone had tried to make sure she got home safely.

She hadn't woken Gus up, because he'd moved his car across the street from the restaurant, and she understood that he hadn't wanted to be discovered. So she'd left him there to awaken in his own time and had thought about him all the way home.

On the drive back to Sara's, her arms and legs had begun to twitch with restless energy. Ideas had come to her, ideas for acting exercises that would encourage bonding and trust. Ideas for skits and improvisations that would let kids use their own greatest gifts.

As each idea came, she had the weirdest sense that Gus was cheering her on.

In high school her grades had been unremarkable; even now it was a sad but true fact that she'd rather watch *Entertainment Tonight* than *20/20*. But Gus's genuine passion for his project and his belief that she could teach his campers made the job appealing for reasons that reached beyond income or proximity to home. Deep inside, Lilah began to yearn for something, a sense of purpose. A place to belong to.

By the time she'd arrived home she knew she was going to take the job. The next day, she left a message on Gus's cell phone. He returned the call, leaving a message for her on Sara's voice mail, inviting her to his place the following week and suggesting she bring Bree to hang out with Elan while the adults talked.

Over the next few days, Lilah spent her time doing two things: driving to the public library in Minot to withdraw books on children's theater, and convincing Bree that going to camp would be fun! Really! She was still engaged in the latter endeavor the day they drove to Gus's house.

"You'll get to hang out with the other kids," she told Bree for what seemed like the hundredth time. "There are going to be classes in archery and Native American drumming!" Infusing her voice with desperate-parent zeal, she tried to remember what else Gus had said on the voice mail. "Oh, yeah, they're going to have wilderness survival training!"

"Oh. My. God." Bree twisted to gape at her. "What kind of demented geek do you think I am? As if learning to pee on a bush is going to, like, help me get into college?"

Lilah couldn't help it—because that sounded like something she would have said, she laughed. Then, because she realized Bree had uttered her first positive statement in days, she asked, "So you're planning to go to college someday?"

A guarded look stole across Bree's face. "My mom wanted me to." She picked at the cover flap of one of the library books she'd checked out. "She said medicine was a really good thing to study if I could get a scholarship."

"It is," Lilah said, "and you can...get a scholarship, I mean. You're very intelligent." Surprised and pleased, she wondered how much she could get for the *Calamity Jane* movie poster she had autographed by Doris Day that was up in Sara's attic. If Bree wanted to study medicine, she would do everything in her power to facilitate that. "Are you thinking about being a doctor or a nurse?"

Bree squirmed in her seat. "Neither. I said my *mom* said it was a good thing to do." She paused then assumed a stubborn expression Lilah recognized only too well. "I'm going to be an actress."

Lilah nearly skidded off the road. "Are you out of your mind?" Easing off the gas and putting both hands firmly on the steering wheel, she warned, "Don't say that. Not even as a joke."

"I'm not joking." Bree's tone acquired more conviction.

"Oh, yeah? Well, neither am I when I say 'Over my dead, has-been body!'"

Bree looked at her curiously then shrugged. "I'm not going to be a has-been. I'm going to do theater, and theater actors can work until they're really old. I watch the Tony awards. I'll probably go to college and get a degree in drama so I can teach if I'm ever out of work, and then I'll go to New York and audition for Broadway."

Admittedly, that was a much better plan than her own idea of going to L.A. to be discovered waiting tables, but Lilah was not reassured. She'd given up everything—everything—to become an actress, for all the wrong reasons, as it turned out, and she would do anything to keep Bree from making the same mistakes.

Before she could come up with dream-dashing reasons that bore logic even an eleven-year-old might understand, Bree announced, "I'll help you teach drama at the camp."

"I beg your pardon?"

"My mom put me in drama class when I was seven. I've been in thrée plays. I've got lots of experience, in case you're thinking I want to ride your coattails or something."

Lilah glanced over, a bittersweet smile rising to her lips. Grace had put Bree in drama class? "No, that's not what I was thinking."

Then she realized something—she and Bree were talking.

"So, you'll go to the camp then?" she asked.

"To help you teach acting." Bree very carefully made that a condition of camp attendance. "And maybe I'll do some of the archery stuff, but I *won't* pee except in a bathroom and I don't want to sleep in a tent."

Lilah pretended to have to think about the terms. "All right. It's a deal."

When Bree turned toward the windshield, a satisfied and even excited smile lurking around her lips, Lilah's heart felt lighter than it had in months.

When acres of tan prairie turned into the lush green of well-irrigated fields, she knew she had reached Gus's land. A large carved wooden sign that said simply, "Hoffman," marked the private drive to his house.

Maneuvering her car down the narrow road, she ignored her perspiring hands. When she reached the house, she was fairly certain she should have brought a change of clothes, because now she was sweating all over.

Gus had built a showplace.

The towering A-frame had floor to ceiling, western-facing windows to take advantage of the sunset. Though portions of the home were still under construction—notably, a large deck Lilah was sure belonged to the master bedroom—the majority of the house was complete.

He had once been ashamed to allow her to see where he lived. She knew well that as a boy he'd never even dreamed of owning a place like this.

"Radical," Bree pronounced the house, staring out her open window.

"Very radical," Lilah agreed.

Parking in front of the three-car garage, she cut the engine, opened her door and stepped out. Bree followed her along crunchy gravel that awaited a landscaper's overhaul and stood by her side, appearing, Lilah thought, a bit intimidated by her surroundings. There was no sound from within the house when Lilah rang the doorbell, but a moment later a dog began to bark, and they heard paws scrambling across hardwood flooring, followed by the stomp and scuff of sneaker-clad feet. A breathless young man opened the door.

"Hi! I'm Elan. Are you Lilah? My dad said you were coming to talk to him. Is this your daughter?" He looked with refreshingly open interest at Bree. "You want to see my room?"

"I'm not her daughter. My mother died. I don't have any parents now. What's so great about your room?"

Lilah retained her smile only with concerted effort. She had a vision of Bree in goth makeup and an obscene number of tongue rings before she turned twelve. "Yes, I'm Lilah. And this is Bree. She lives with me, and… we're becoming a family." From the corner of her eye, she saw Bree grow bug-eyed and open her mouth, probably to refute any interest in a familial connection.

"No matter where he is in this house, my son manages to reach the door before I do."

Gus's approach managed to forestall an incriminating comment from Bree. Lilah found herself speechless, as well. The sight of him in his jeans and a clean, untucked gray T-shirt that skimmed over his muscular build threatened to stop her heart. He was simply unlike any other man she knew. The T-shirt mirrored the rock-gray of his eyes. His skin and hair were gold as wheat. Without trying, he looked like some mythical being who'd emerged from the earth and never forgot he was part of it.

He was also engaged, and right now Lilah considered that a safety net.

"I've got a new horse," he told the preteens watching him, "a three-year-old mare, being delivered in about fifteen minutes. The two of you might want to watch her being unloaded."

Try as she might, Bree could not disguise her interest. Eyes full of desire, she turned toward Lilah. "Can I?"

The question emerged in a mumble, no doubt about it, but was a seminal moment for their relationship; the first time Bree actually asked her permission to do something. *As if I'm a mom.*

Gratitude rose in Lilah. "Sure, honey." The endearment slipped out, but Lilah decided quickly that it belonged in the air, hovering however awkwardly. They had to begin somewhere.

Elan, perhaps the only member of their little party who felt no tension at all, grinned beautifully, all white teeth and caramel skin and unconditional friendship. He spoke to Bree, his body primed to shoot through the front door. "Follow me!"

Bree did, and Lilah was left alone with Gus in the

spacious foyer. Against her chest she held a binder filled with notes, so that she felt pretty much the way she had at fourteen, spying him in the hallway at school, feeling her heart speed up and her mind slow way down as she tried to hide her awareness. There'd been water under the bridge then, too, but now the water was deeper. As dramatic and complicated as her attraction had felt in high school, she could multiply the drama a hundred times now and still underestimate the impact of the past on her present relationship with Gus.

And yet, she knew it was time to change his opinion of her. She began by demonstrating that she wasn't the attention-seeking airhead he remembered.

"I have quite a few notes to show you. Dimensions and prospective costs for an inexpensive proscenium stage we could build in scene shop. Sample lesson plans for the acting component of the program. I Googled some information on Alexander Technique, too, because movement and vocal lessons would be beneficial for kids Bree and Elan's age, don't you think?"

"Do you want to see the new mare?"

"Beg your pardon?"

His gray eyes twinkled as if he were lighthearted, something she'd rarely associated with Gus. "If I remember correctly, you were as horse crazy as I was," he reminded her. "Your ideas sound good. We can sit down and chat after I show you around, acquaint you with the lay of the land."

"Oh. If that's the way you want to do it. Okay. Sure."

Good Lord, she was nervous. She'd prepared a brief presentation but he'd thrown her off her script. She nearly squealed when he pulled the notebook from her arms.

"Why don't we leave this here?" He placed the notebook on a handsomely carved table in the eatery. "You won't have to carry it."

Her mind knew they'd traveled too far to turn back; her heart, however, had amnesia, and his smile could have melted her like butter if she allowed it.

Following him out the door, she kept her distance and kept her wits about her. "I love these steps. Is the rock from around here?"

"Mmm-hmm."

"Great view. It was a good choice to face the house in this direction."

"Yes."

"You'll enjoy a lot of sunsets. You and your family."

"Undoubtedly."

All the way to the corral Gus had constructed a good quarter mile from the house, she maintained a commentary intended to be friendly, upbeat and as impersonal as possible. For a short walk, she managed to refer quite a few times to "your family" and each time was sure her inflection suggested that she was one-hundred-percent at peace with the fact that he'd moved on in his life.

Bree and Elan were already perched on the top fence rail when she and Gus arrived. Hopping down from the cab of a truck hauling a horse trailer, a deeply tanned man with a craggy face beamed in Gus's direction. "Just in time! She's been making noises to get out of there."

Gus headed over to shake hands and share a few words. Lilah joined Bree and Elan at the fence.

With her long brown hair streaming behind her and her gaze glued to the mare that was snorting in the trailer, Bree looked more interested and more relaxed than Lilah had ever seen her. She looked like a kid instead of a beleaguered adult or an isolated teen.

The hairs on Lilah's arms rose as Gus leaned on the fence rail, next to her.

"Spirited, isn't she?"

Lilah could hardly focus on the horse. Though she hadn't turned to look at him, her senses were filled with Gus and only Gus. Gazing beyond the horse, she took in the acres of prairie that comprised his property. Rugged, gentle with an infinite variety of subtle beauties, the prairie reminded her of Gus. They shared a certain purity, an integrity, a sometimes austere challenge that welcomed only those brave enough to stay.

I wish I'd been brave enough. I wish I could do it all over again.

In a world where do-overs were actually possible, Lilah would stay and support Gus; she would be wise enough to understand that fear more than hope propelled her flight to California and that actions arising from fear seldom ended well.

But who was that smart at seventeen? You snooze, you lose, and she'd lost the man who held the missing piece of her soul. It was a truth written across the midnight sky, and neither time nor mistakes changed the truth.

She turned her head, felt the breeze blowing away the muck of the past, at least for this moment, and when she found Gus looking at her, she returned the gaze steadily. In the corral, the mare whinnied, tossed her head, stamped the ground.

"She's beautiful, Gus. Wild enough to make things interesting. She fits in this prairie. So do you."

Surprise, then satisfaction, lit his eyes, and he nodded. "I've definitely come full circle. There's something inherently right about that." He searched her face. "What about you, Lilah? Is this just a pit stop for you? Will North Dakota ever be home again?"

Tears caught her off guard. Quickly slipping her sunglasses from the top of her head to the bridge of her nose, she affected the breezy laugh that used to come much more easily. "Oh, I don't think so."

Another woman would share this land and the home he'd built...and his children. Another woman would watch the sunsets and hold tight to the heart Lilah had fumbled. She could accept all that, because she had to; but she no longer wanted to lie to herself about how much it would hurt.

"I'm sure I'll be back often, though, for visits." Stealing a peek at Bree, who was clearly enjoying herself for the first time since Grace took ill, Lilah knew Kalamoose would, of necessity, be her vacation destination for years to come.

She knew, too, that the time for confessions was rapidly approaching.

"Why don't we leave the kids—they'll be fine—and head back to the house to discuss business? As long as you're planning on staying through the summer, we can use your help with the camp."

"I'm planning on being here."

Advising Elan to look after Bree and to ask the housekeeper for something to eat and drink when they were ready, Gus led Lilah back to the house.

Once there, he settled her in the living room then headed to the kitchen for a word with his house-keeper, Loida. He returned with a tray bearing two glasses of lemonade, a plate of warm cornbread and a small glass bowl filled with what she knew immediately was raspberry jam.

Lemonade, cornbread and raspberry jam—she'd had it for lunch, she'd had it as a snack. It had been her favorite combination of flavors in high school. The ultimate happy meal. Since this couldn't be a coincidence, she didn't mask her surprise.

"I haven't eaten this stuff since I started my first diet."

"You don't need to diet." He spoke matter-of-factly, with no intent to flatter.

"Tell that to the Hollywood casting directors."

With their snack set on the coffee table, Gus sank onto the large chenille sofa. "Do you really care what they think?"

"I'm supposed to."

He raised a brow, and her response seemed to matter to him. "Do you?"

Glancing around the room at the furniture he—and probably his fiancée—had chosen with obvious care, Lilah knew once more that it was over for her and Gus; impressing him with her answer wouldn't change anything.

"After this summer, I have to get serious about my career again. Or get serious about some other career," she said, thinking out loud. "I need to make a living, and all I've ever wanted to do is act. All I've ever *tried* to do is act. Well, act and wait tables." She smiled wryly. The truth didn't bother her as much as it would have even a few months ago.

"You've acted in a few things. I saw *Attack Girls on Planet Venus.*"

"Oh, no!" she groaned. And then she realized… "You did? The movie didn't make it into theaters."

"I know. I looked you up on the Internet and rented the video."

That was almost as surprising as his remembering her passion for cornbread and jam. "Were you looking for a laugh?" She frowned, picturing the scene: Gus and a few friends: *Can you believe I used to date her? Third attack girl from the left, the one in the shredded bikini.*

"I was looking up an old friend," he countered evenly, "and wanted to know whether she was living her dream." Lilah didn't know what to say, so he asked point blank, "Were you?"

Lilah considered how she'd been living over the past

ten years. Padding her resume, having her hair and nails done before she saw her sisters, eating shredded wheat and popcorn so she could spend two months' worth of grocery money on tooth whitening—all lies, all desperate attempts to feel like someone else. Someone special. "Me, only better," she used to say. But "better" had never been good enough.

In truth, she was a sometimes-lonely, almost thirty-year-old who missed her family and was bone-weary. The dream—it was all about feeling loved. Not even *being* loved, because the truth was her family had always loved her. Gus had loved her. It hadn't been enough. The hunt for more—more success, more acceptance, more admiration—had left her so much emptier than before.

"No, I wasn't living my dream," she admitted. "As it turns out, it wasn't the right one." Before he could react, she admitted, "I looked you up on the Internet, too."

"To discover whether I was living my dream?"

To discover whether you were married. But she didn't say that. "This summer camp," she pressed on, deciding business was the only safe topic left, "it sounds like something you've been planning a long time."

"It is." Stretching out his arms, he leaned back against the sofa, able to relax and at the same time look at her so intently that she felt chills. "I want to hear your idea for the theater classes. You arrived with notes. Tell me what you're thinking."

For the next fifteen minutes, Lilah described her

plans. She began hesitantly, but gathered steam as she warmed once more to the ideas she'd compiled and as Gus leaned forward to listen. "Rather than using material that's already available, I'd like the kids to write their own scenes. That way they can work on something that has meaning for them, experience a real sense of creative control and expression."

"I like that idea. I like it very much. But some of these kids are below grade level in school. I don't know what their writing skills will be."

"Well, I thought about that, because my writing skills weren't the best, either," Lilah conceded. "And I thought the camp counselors or adult volunteers could help. You might be able to cull from local writers' groups."

He nodded. "That would be great for their self-esteem."

They talked on, Lilah sharing what she'd come up with so far and Gus adding to her ideas, making her more excited about them than before. By the time Lilah looked at her watch, an hour had passed. She swung her gaze toward the floor-to-ceiling windows.

"Where are the kids?"

"I heard them come through the kitchen door about twenty minutes ago. My guess is they're on the patio, making a sizable dent in a chocolate cake that Loida was frosting." Gus stretched his arms overhead.

"You heard them come in? I didn't. Some mother I'm turning out to—" She clipped the last word when she realized what she'd said.

Gus took the stray comment in stride. "I had trouble thinking of myself as Elan's father at first. Then he asked if he could call me 'Dad.' Makes a big difference. It's usually awkward in the beginning. How are you and Bree getting on these days?"

Anxiety chomped into her relaxation. Lilah laughed awkwardly. "She doesn't want me to be 'Mom,' if that's what you mean."

Presented with an opening to discuss Bree in more depth, she should have jumped on it. Weeks ago, Lilah began to note that Bree shared many of Grace's mannerisms. Lately, however, she'd begun to see how very much Bree shared Sara's physicality. Same nose, which Sara had inherited from their Grandma Owens, same stubbornly square chin and lanky limbs that would remain slim for life. Gus had already mentioned the resemblance once. Was it merely a matter of time before he mentioned it again and questioned the unlikelihood of a coincidence? Even Sara, who rarely noticed a mug that wasn't on an FBI Most Wanted poster, had begun to do double takes at Bree.

Lilah knew it would be better by far to initiate the inevitable confession rather than to wait for someone to confront her. And yet, coward that she was, she jumped from the sofa as if it had grown teeth and bitten her butt. She walked across the large room to a large cabinet that displayed two gorgeous handblown glass pieces and an exquisite bronze sculpture.

"These colors match the room," she observed lamely,

while another portion of her brain tried to deduce what her mouth ought to be saying. "Did you hire a decorator?"

"No."

Just got engaged to a woman with really good taste, eh?

While her stomach sank, her speech sped up. "I admire women who can decorate. It's not my forte. My apartment in L.A. was abundant in dried flower arrangements. I thought they'd give the place a garden feel."

Behind her, still on the sofa, Gus laughed, which somehow spurred her toward new heights in Awkward Attempts To Learn About The Fiancée. "You're lucky," she trilled, looking at the bronze sculpture as if she were speaking to it rather than Gus. "You'll be married to someone who can decorate your next fifty years together. No fear of dueling Barcaloungers in your old age. Everyone should be so lucky."

Gus appeared at her side, joining in her overzealous perusal of his knickknacks. "I chose the glass and bronze," he corrected. "Karen isn't much for decorating, either."

"Oh. Too bad," Lilah murmured.

"Yeah." Still facing forward, Gus nodded contemplatively. "I might wind up with Barcaloungers, after all. Not with Karen, though."

He said it so low, Lilah had to ask him to repeat himself. For the reprise, he turned fully toward her. "My engagement is over. Nobody's fault." He paused, then amended, "Mine, probably. For not finishing one chapter before I began another."

Lilah faced him. She didn't want to read into his words, but she needed answers to the questions careening around her mind like slap happy pinballs.

"Are you saying you need closure in your relationship with me? And that when you get it, you can move on?"

His expression tightened. "I'm saying I've never had closure with you. And that maybe there's a reason."

"What…what reason?"

He shook his head. "I don't know."

They were standing closer than they had in years and years. Lilah grew dizzy on aftershave, pheromones and, for the first time since she'd arrived home, hope.

Gus lifted a hand toward her face. Her breath quickened…his hand lowered. Disappointment sucked her down to earth like a vacuum until he said, "I don't know anything except that it's not over for me. Not yet." And then he did touch her, a brush of her arm she might have passed off as her imagination except that his fingers lingered at her wrist. A thousand waves broke in her ears when he asked, "Is it over for you?"

Hope beat again, strong like a hungry eagle, jittery like the prey. Lilah thought of Bree, of her family, of Elan. She thought of the patch job she'd done on her own heart the first time it had broken. Would there be anything left to hold together if Gus wound up hating her once the truth was out? It might be easier—for everyone—if she let sleeping dogs lie. She could pack Bree up, head back to L.A. or to a new city, find a job, begin again. Cut the ties that bound her to the mistakes of her past.

The past closed gently around her wrist and squeezed, asking again, *Is it over for you?*

The truth was so obvious. And the temptation so strong. "No. It's never been over."

Chapter Thirteen

Bree let Lilah tuck her in for the first time.

Well, Lilah admitted, getting a glass of water from the kitchen tap and staring at nothing out the window above the sink, perhaps "tuck in" was a wee exaggeration. But she didn't object when Lilah came in to wish her a good night's sleep. That had been an hour ago, at eleven. Sara was sleeping at the jail tonight, having picked up a drunken Owen Bristol at Stone's Throw Tavern—so named because it was a stone's throw from everything else in town—and was attempting to deliver him to his own house. Owen had been getting pie eyed twice a month like clockwork for as long as Lilah could remember. According to the ritual, Owen would go to the tavern, drink too much, then kick up a fuss when the sheriff—first Uncle Harm and now Sara—tried to take him home. Owen's wife, Althea, had passed on some thirty-odd years ago and Owen needed the company. So he and the sheriff would head to the jail, play several rounds of checkers and eventually fall asleep on the cell cots. Owen always left before sunrise, no harm done except for the discomfort of sleeping on a thin, lumpy mattress.

Sara never complained about this custom she'd inherited with the job, and she never tried to end it. It was one of the few purely sweet things that she did, at least that anyone knew about.

Lilah knew she'd be alone with her thoughts for the rest of the night. Draining the glass of lukewarm water quickly enough to give herself a stomachache, she replayed, for the umpteenth time, her afternoon with Gus.

Right on cue, the kids had stampeded into the house, forcing a postponement of the conversation. Stepping between Gus and Lilah, Elan had raced up to beg, "Dad, can we go swimming?"

Because Bree had no bathing suit, it was determined that swimming would have to wait. Then, as the kids were clearly intent on hanging around, Lilah and Gus adjourned their meeting. Gus gave her a to-go package of cornbread and jam, and that was that.

But the past had irreversibly rushed forward to greet the present, and now changes—the big, unavoidable kind—were around the bend.

Setting her glass in the sink, she glanced at the clock and wondered what to do with herself. Six minutes past midnight. That left a good six hours until sunrise, time during which she would have to find a way to calm the storm in her mind or be swept away by a fury of what if's and what now's, of asking herself over and over whether she should tell the truth the moment she saw him again or steal just a few moments of growing closer.

The decision was made the moment she saw the car cruise up and park across the road.

Breathing as if she'd walked five miles in below zero weather, the back of her throat stinging with each inhalation, she watched Gus walk toward the house, his silhouette growing bigger and more distinct with every step. Shaking, hands fumbling with the knob, she opened the kitchen door and waited.

They met on the porch as if it was what they'd done every night for the past dozen years.

"You're late." Lilah's whisper was sweet and soft as cotton candy, a girl's whisper.

"You knew I'd be coming?"

She shook her head. "Not until I saw you park across the street. Then it seemed…"

He reached for her. No mistaking his touch this time, his hand cupping her face, his thumb stroking her cheek before he slipped his fingers into the hair at her nape and urged her closer. "Inevitable?"

She nodded. "Yes." His nose and lips and chin seemed more perfect and more precious than any bronze, and his eyes… They held her, drawing her as close as his hands did. And then, before any secrets could be told or regrets expressed, they were kissing. It was the first kiss they'd shared as two legal adults with every right to each other, and it was the best one they'd ever shared, their desire made bottomless by years of waiting and wishing.

They explored each other so tenderly at first, holding their hunger at bay as they made sure they both wanted the same thing.

"Where's Elan?" Lilah breathed when they broke apart.

"Loida lives in." Gus kept his head close to hers. "Bree?"

"Sleeping upstairs."

"Your sister?"

"At the jail." She paused. "All night."

She felt Gus tense, his breath held. There was a downstairs bedroom Harm used to use when he came home late and didn't want to wake the girls by climbing the creaking staircase. Gus no doubt remembered the room, because on nights when Harm was already ensconced on the second floor and Lilah's sisters were also safely asleep, she would climb out the window of that well-located bedroom.

"Does the window still stick?" he asked, threading more intimacy and a smile through the moment.

"I haven't tried it in a long, long time."

She reached for his hand. Their fingers found each other, linking together in a reminder that simple handholding could ignite the fire between them.

All the reasons they should talk first and touch later crowded into Lilah's mind. She pushed them away.

There weren't many second chances. She'd thought, absolutely, that she'd lost hers. Now Gus was here, and for once the present seemed more important than the past. Her fingers faltered, loosened their grip for a moment, but he held on...and on. His gray eyes flashed like lightening. There would be a reckoning tomorrow, a storm of a different kind, but whatever Lilah had to face, whatever they both had to face, tonight they would stand in the path of the twister and revel in its force.

Tonight, there would be one more midnight.

She awakened at four according to the old clock whose hands still lurched valiantly by the side of the bed. Before her eyes fully opened, Lilah knew Gus was gone. The room felt empty.

Her heart, however, was as full as it had ever been.

Making love to Gus had always felt thrilling, tender, exhausting and exhilarating all at once. That hadn't changed. Little had, except that he took more time, made every moment count; and she became more assertive, intent on exploring every aspect of a lovemaking that would never be as powerful with anyone as it was with him.

Reaching for the lamp, she blinked, rolled over and found a note written on a pale blue page he'd torn from the pad in the kitchen:

Will you come to my place for lunch tomorrow? The kids can swim, we can talk. Noon, unless I hear from you. I'll ask Loida to make tuna on rye with a side of cheese puffs, baked not fried.

Gus

P.S. I remember everything about you.

If it was possible to tingle everywhere, Lilah did. Gus...*Gus.* She wasn't going to even attempt not to love him. If she could just borrow a little more time... If she knew he loved her again, too, then maybe they would work everything out. And they would live together, in his house or anywhere. They would raise a family...but midnights would belong to the two of them...forever and ever...and ever...

Turning off the lamp, she rolled to her side, hugging the pillow and the note. She hoped sleep would come again so the sweetness would linger, easier still in the velvet night than by the light of day.

Tomorrow would bring the need for truth and integrity, but tonight...tonight she wanted to snuggle into the dream.

At ten minutes to noon, Gus felt as if he were about to entertain the queen of England rather than his high school girlfriend...

...current lover...

...the love of his life.

The magic of holding Lilah in his arms again told

him all he needed to know: they never should have said goodbye.

Setting purchased flowers in the middle of the dining table, he stepped back, trying to see his home the way she might. The practice was nothing new. With every one of his achievements in the past decade, with every piece of framing that had gone up in this house, every chair or table or sofa he'd brought in, he'd wondered, "What would Lilah think?"

Of course, those musings had been fueled by resentment. Today was different, delightfully so. Today, he was a man who wanted his woman to be proud.

"How come we're eating lunch in the dining room?" Elan looked at the table, set formally for four. Disappointment showed clearly on his face. "I thought we were going to eat outside by the pool. I'm going to show Bree how to cannonball like a guy. Girls can't do it. They don't know how to make a big splash."

Gus laughed at his son, his pleasure absolutely unadulterated for the first time in years. "Some girls do, son. You just have to know the right ones."

"You know a girl who can cannonball?"

"Well, I—" The doorbell rang. Loida hustled out from the kitchen. "That's all right, I've got it." Elan raced to the door ahead of him. "*We've* got it," Gus amended, following his son from the room. He didn't mind admitting—to himself, of course—that a flurry of butterflies beat in his stomach as he approached the door.

One look at Lilah, dressed in a pink T-shirt with red

lettering that stated First Lady and jeans that made her legs look a mile long, and the butterflies flew nonstop to his heart. Grinning like a damn fool, he reached her just as she tilted her head and answered Elan. "What do you mean, 'cannonball'?"

"It's a kind of dive," Bree answered for Elan. "I can do it better than he does, but he doesn't believe me."

"How do you know you can do it better if you've never seen mine?" Elan protested.

"How about we welcome our guests and call them liars later?" Gus entered the foyer with an apologetic smile, directed mostly at Lilah.

Her gaze immediately shifted to his. Had Elan and Bree been any older, they might have felt the change in the air. Because they were engrossed in a discussion about who might be the best cannonballer ever, they missed the sparks that flew between the adults.

Gus moved closer, speaking over the kids' heads. "Welcome back."

Lilah's smile, the same glowing beacon that made her every boy's fantasy, was his and his alone today. "Same to you."

It didn't take long at all for Gus to decide that Elan was right. A picnic around the pool sounded just right— for the kids. Summoning his housekeeper, he asked her to supervise them in packing their lunches to go. Then he asked Elan to show Bree where she could put on her bathing suit and drew Lilah into the dining room for a glass of chilled Chablis.

"I loved your ideas the other day. Did I tell you that?"

Sipping from the goblet he handed her, she smiled into her glass. "You mentioned it, yes."

"They're bright. Innovative. Appropriate for the kids we're trying to help. I made a good choice in hiring you."

Lilah stared at Gus a moment, then allowed her smile to grow as big as it wanted. Which was very big. And bright. And surprisingly winsome. "Are you trying to unnerve me?"

"No. I'm trying to tell you that your intelligence and creativity are as much a turn on as your—" he glanced at the red type across her bosom "—slogans."

Her eyes twinkled, but then she asked very seriously, "You really think my ideas will work?"

Though he wanted to take her into his arms right there, Gus kept his hands to himself, allowing only a sober nod. "I do."

She flushed with pleasure, and he realized that he used to assume her popularity and confidence walked hand in hand. She'd been in her element in high school, where she'd relied on her looks. It startled him to realize she had less faith in her mind and talents. He was going to enjoy working with her this summer, watching her bloom, learning more and more about Lilah the woman.

In fact, investigating the lovely, unknown creature before him was so tempting, he hardly minded sitting down to lunch instead of taking her into his bedroom and making love until every moment they'd spent apart faded from memory.

Gus took her to visit the new mare after lunch. They'd chatted about the summer camp and his plans for the ranch all through the meal, clinking glasses to toast each other's ideas and laughing when the cheese puffs turned their fingers fluorescent orange.

They didn't kiss, didn't even come close, though they spent a lot of time eyeing each other's lips, and in a way that was as exciting. Lilah felt as if she were in a dream. A dangerous dream in which she and Gus could begin from here, no questions asked, no pasts rehashed, no secrets unearthed. Just two people who'd discovered that no one else would do.

At the corral, the nervous mare shied away. Gus gentled her simply by placing one of his large hands on the bridge between her eyes and speaking in tender tones, as if she were a family member rather than a horse. The mare fell a little in love, and Lilah sank deeper, too.

By the time they reached the pool, where the kids were splashing each other and everything else, Lilah had begun to feel that everything in her world was right for the first time in her adult life. And even though she knew she and Gus had to talk, that it was wrong to postpone the inevitable, she dearly wanted this one day to revel in the feeling of belonging, both to this place and to these people.

While she sat on a deck chair, laughing at the kids'

incessant dare-you's, Gus excused himself to head for the kitchen. He returned ten minutes later with a plate of cookies Loida had just pulled from the oven.

"Sugar!" he called to the wildly splashing kids. "Come kill your appetites for dinner."

Setting the cookies on the umbrella-covered table where Lilah had seated herself, he stood near her chair, his pheromones as distracting outdoors as they were in. His hip level with her head, he folded muscular arms and waited while the kids chased each other out of the pool.

Both he and Lilah kept their eyes on the pair of laughing, wet preteens, who in two days had reached the point of teasing and bickering as if they'd been raised together. With Gus hovering by her chair, it could have been a typical domestic scene. A day out of any family's summer.

"Oh, no! Peanut butter." Elan moaned, picking up a cookie and sniffing it loudly. He wagged his head in disappointment.

"What's wrong with peanut butter? That's my favorite!" Bree reached for a cookie and took a big, crumbly bite. "Yum. They're warm."

"Yuck. They're peanut butter."

"Yum, they're peanut butter."

"Yuck."

"*Yum.*" She rolled her eyes. "You don't have any taste at all."

"*Yuck.* You don't even know what's good."

Bree made a big show of eating and *loving* the cookie. Elan countered by pretending to throw up.

"You two need psychiatric help." Gus shook his head. "You remind me of—"

He stopped himself. Elan and Bree didn't know what he'd been about to say, but Lilah had no doubt. And she agreed; their children bickered just the way they had.

"*I* was never argumentative," she stated, making Gus laugh so hard she thought he might collapse a lung.

"Did you bring a bathing suit, Ms. Owens?" he asked. "So we can show these young people the right and wrong way to freestyle swim?"

She gave him exactly the response he wanted— hands on hips and her expression outraged. "I hope you're not implying that my freestyle is anything but graceful. Although I do recall that your form had a certain choppiness."

The kids were enjoying every minute of the banter. Gus grinned. "Suit up, Ms. Owens, and let a pro show you how to stroke the water."

The next two hours passed in a joyful cacophony of splashes, shouts and laughter that made Lilah feel so buoyant she was sure she could float without trying. Finally she pleaded exhaustion and spread a towel over one of the lounge chairs surrounding the pool. Then she spread out another towel, deciding she and Bree should be going home soon, as they were supposed to meet Sara for dinner. When she said as much, however, there were protests all around, including a dive beneath the water from Bree.

When she resurfaced briefly for air, Lilah commanded, "Hold it! We need to go, so you have to start getting ready. You can lie in the sun for a few minutes."

Bree protested until Elan said he'd lie in the sun with her. They spread their towels out over two pool chairs. He flopped onto his stomach; she, on her back.

Gus pulled himself from the pool and came to lie beside Lilah. Grabbing her sunglasses, she slipped them on and lay back in the lounger, deciding not to watch his advance. Well, maybe she peeked a *little*. Her goose bumps were not due to cold.

"She's got a lot of spirit," he said quietly to Lilah as he lowered himself to the chair beside hers. Bree and Elan had just embarked on a conversation about Olympic gold medalist swimmers, and Bree challenged Elan to a swimming match next time she came over.

Lilah nodded. "She's needed it. Sometimes it's scary, because she attacks the simplest things like a game that has to be won."

"Reminds me of someone else," he murmured, and Lilah looked up.

"Me?" she asked, genuinely surprised. "I didn't do that."

One golden brow rose. "Cheerleading? Beauty pageants? You waged a campaign for the junior high homecoming court that would have made George Stephanopoulis green with envy."

"Well, I liked to win."

"I know." He hitched his chin toward Bree, who had

rolled onto her side and was now *betting* Elan she would beat him if they raced.

A low chuckle rumbled from Gus. "You and she are actually a lot alike. She does that same dare-me head toss you used to do."

"She does?" Only Gus could say something simple and start a flood of complex emotions.

"You must be rubbing off on her," he speculated.

"Yeah. Poor kid." It was time to go. *Now.* Lilah wanted the memory of this day, if only this one day, just as it was. And everyone was getting along so well. If they could have just a little more time to enjoy the sunshine before the inevitable winds of change. "Come on, Bree. You can finish drying off in the car."

Bree was too deep into bickering to hear. Lilah glanced at Gus. Had the sun been higher, she'd have guessed he was squinting because of it. But it was four p.m. and even though it was still warm, the light was not ungentle. His expression, however, was beginning to grow a bit…harsh.

Following the line of his gaze to Bree's back, Lilah felt her blood freeze.

In a bikini instead of her usual tank swimsuit, Bree's midback was exposed, and—

Oh, my lord. Lilah blinked. It shouldn't have surprised her, really, but—

Fingers wrapped around Lilah's wrist, squeezing like handcuffs a size too small. She looked at Gus. He never glanced her way, but his expression was thunderous.

To the kids, he called, "We'll be right back." If they heard, they didn't care, too immersed in their own discussion.

Still without a word or glance, and without releasing the pressure on her wrist, he tugged Lilah from the chair and led her around the house, to a side entrance she had never before used.

Lilah's stomach went sick with nerves. She'd seen the same thing he had when she'd followed his gaze to Bree. It might have made her feel good had she not realized when she felt his grip that an explanation was going to be necessary.

Gus propelled her ahead of him into what was obviously his office. When he let her go, her wrist burned. One look at his eyes, and her face burned, too.

Betrayal. Gus glared at her with a look of betrayal so black and outraged it nearly stopped her breath.

He opened the discussion with a nasty swear word. "How could you do it? I asked you who she was, and you lied!" Swearing again, he demanded, "All these years?" His face filled with red-hot rage, and his volume escalated with every word. "It didn't bother you to know that every day, every minute you kept silent, you were stealing another day from me? Robbing me of the chance to know my own daughter?"

An awful bitterness filled Lilah's mouth. She swallowed it and tried to speak, but Gus took two swift steps to close the gap between them then grabbed her shoulders and hauled her forward. He growled into her face.

"Is that why you're back now? You want money… child support…what? What made you decide it was finally time to tell me? No, wait. I'll take a wild guess: Your sister told you I wasn't the mangy kid from the wrong side of the tracks, anymore. Now that I've got money you're willing to renew old acquaintances. Is that what last night was about?"

"No! Stop it, Gus, you don't understand the situation—"

"I understand everything I need to! Don't deny it again," he warned, "I saw the birthmark."

The birthmark—pale, café au lait and unevenly shaped—decorated Bree's lower back, the way Lilah's decorated hers. As if they'd gotten matching tattoos.

When Lilah first saw it—the same time as Gus— she'd felt a swift rush of gladness…almost joy. The birthmark was proof, even when she wasn't getting along with Bree, even when she felt like a failure as a parent, that she was indeed this child's mother. Bree didn't look like her. Bree didn't really like her. But they were connected, and somehow they would make it work, because in a timeless way they belonged to each other.

The way Bree and Gus belonged.

He was so angry right now, and though she didn't blame him—how could she—he wasn't remembering all the chaos of their lives at the time they'd conceived their daughter. "If you calm down, I'll explain every—"

"Calm down?" His lips curled back derisively. He shook his head. "What a jackass I've been. For years everything I did, everything I became was about impressing you. I had you in the back of my mind, like a target I kept trying to reach. I didn't even know where you were." Unconsciously his fingers pressed into her shoulders hard enough to cause pain. "I never stopped thinking about you, and that makes me a prize idiot. When the hell were you thinking of me? *You hid my daughter from me.* You lied every day that she was with you."

Lilah began to panic that Bree would hear them, that she would discover one of the most important pieces of her life in an utterly wrong way. And though Lilah still hadn't figured out what the right way was, she knew that listening to one's birth parents hurl accusations at each other was not it.

"Bree hasn't been with me," she began, keeping her voice and emotions as even as possible. "Only the last couple of months. What I told you before is the truth— her mother, Grace, died and that's when I met Bree again for the first time since—" Lilah's voice began to break. She swallowed and controlled herself with effort. "I hadn't seen her since the first day in the hospital."

Gus had turned away. It was impossible to tell what he was thinking, or what he needed to know. So Lilah began with what she hoped he'd take as reassurances.

"Grace was a good friend. We agreed an adoption would be best for all of us. I knew she'd be a wonderful mother—"

"Bree had a mother!" Gus whipped around, no attempt to modulate his outrage. "And a father. So when you were deciding on adoption, did you think about that? Weren't there papers I was supposed to sign? Or did you tell them you didn't know who the father was?"

Not once did he question that Bree was his. That was something, Lilah supposed. At least he wasn't accusing her of cheating on him. "The father was in jail, Gus." Sadness more than defensiveness infused her words. "In jail and going to prison. You refused to see me and you refused to talk to Uncle Harm. I'm not sure I'd have told you the truth, anyway," she said softly, honestly. "How could the two of us have been decent parents to a little baby? Our own lives were a wreck. I'd graduated with rotten grades, and you missed finals and hadn't graduated at all. I couldn't do that to her. Plus, I was terrified—"

"You were terrified? How do you think I felt sitting in a jail cell, knowing the only good thing in my life got so loused up. Maybe if you—" He stopped himself, exhaling forcefully and lowering his head. When he finally looked up again, his eyes seemed ancient. "Did you know you were pregnant that day I overheard you with your friends?"

"No. I should have realized, I suppose, but…no."

Neither of them was sure it made a lick of difference today—they were both different people—but the heat of Gus's immediate rage dimmed.

"So what now, Lilah? How much does she…Bree…" He said the word differently, as if testing it for the first time. "How much does she know?"

"She doesn't know about any of it yet. She knows she

was adopted; that's all. She hasn't asked me about her birth mother yet. To her, Grace was Mom and that's that. She doesn't like me much, in case you hadn't noticed."

There were endless matters to discuss. They both knew it. For now, though, Gus wanted to make only one thing clear. "I want her in my life. In my home. If you're planning to leave Kalamoose again and to take Bree with you, I'll fight you on it."

So long happily ever after.

Sorrow rose inside Lilah. Not for bringing Bree into the world. And not for making an adoption plan that gave her daughter the best possible chance at a loving and secure beginning. Rather, Lilah's sorrow stemmed from her inability to provide that beginning....

Sorrow that she and Gus hadn't been able to hold each other and rock their daughter while they made monumental decisions about her future.

The eyes that had spent two days devouring her now shifted as if he'd turn to stone if he glanced in her direction.

"Five years," he muttered then laughed roughly. "Five years—that's how long I waited for you to come back. I couldn't look at another woman. Couldn't imagine it. And then for years after that..." He shook his head. "Ah, what difference does it make now? I ought to be relieved."

Raking his fingers through his hair like a man with thoughts he wanted to purge from his brain, he glared again. "You're sure Bree has no idea you're her—"

She helped him out when he stumbled over the terminology. "Birth mother. No, Sabrina doesn't know. Grace and I agreed to a partially open adoption. I had pictures of Bree, but I'd never seen her until Grace got sick. At the time we worked out the details of the adoption, I thought I was doing it for Bree and Grace's sake…."

"But?"

"But looking back I think I may have chosen not to see her, because I was afraid I couldn't handle it if she…" Lilah felt tears clog her throat. She'd never talked about this out loud to anyone. "I didn't think I could handle it if she hated me for giving her up. I never knew how to explain that I loved her, I just wasn't strong enough to be the mother I knew she needed."

Gus maintained eye contact for a protracted moment, then looked down again. Away from her.

Lilah felt suddenly as if she were the only soul in the room. She wanted him to understand, but perhaps there were some things a person simply could not explain. Some human hurts that time and the truth couldn't wash away.

A knock on the door, the one leading into the house, startled them both so much they actually jerked.

Gus turned. "Come in."

Pushing open the door, Gus's housekeeper, Loida, stood hesitantly on the threshold. A small, slender woman with deeply tanned skin and an attractively well-worn face, her usually open features looked pinched and troubled. "This room is right next to the kitchen," she began without preamble. "The children came in to get something to drink."

She didn't have to say any more. Gus paled, and Lilah's heart began to pound.

Gus crossed toward Loida. "Did you hear it all?" he asked, his voice a hoarse scratch.

The housekeeper gave a jerky nod. "Most. I tried to shoo them out." She shook her head, appearing almost as distressed as the parents. "Elan is with her in the living room."

Lilah felt rather than saw Gus turn toward her. She acted immediately, her first thought for Bree.

Muttering, "Thank you, Loida," she passed through the door. Without a backward glance toward Gus, Lilah forced her courage to enfold her fear and hurried to face her daughter.

Chapter Fourteen

Trying to speak with Bree on the car ride back to Sara's was simply a mistake. Silent and trembling, with her arms folded tightly around herself and her lips pressed together, Bree flatly refused to talk, and she acted as if she didn't hear a word Lilah said.

So Lilah talked *at* her. She told Bree she loved her, that although she realized it was hard to understand, she had always loved the baby who had begun life as her daughter. She explained that that kind of love never goes away. And then she told Bree that they were going to have to talk this through and find a way for Lilah to make amends, because she planned to be in Bree's life from now on, every day, in one way or another.

When Lilah asked whether Bree had any questions about Gus, Bree's skinny arms wrapped so tightly around herself, Lilah's heart nearly broke. Obviously there was no end to the mistaken way she and probably Grace, too, had handled the situation. *I'll make it up to you, Bree. I'll be honest every day for the rest of my life. I'll hire a team of therapists. I'll call Oprah.* She and Gus would work together to make sure Bree knew how loved and special and wanted she was. It would just take time.

Sick with grief and nerves despite her pep talk to herself, Lilah noticed immediately upon arriving at Sara's the shiny new car, a Volvo, parked next to the squad car in front of the house. She used a bit too much force to engage the parking brake.

Of all things they didn't need right now, company topped the list.

Bree was out of the car in a flash, racing up the porch steps before Lilah had even opened her door. With heavy legs and a pounding head, she followed.

As she entered the living room, she heard Sara. "Hi, kid. Glad you're back. Supper's on in a half hour. Nettie's cooking."

Nettie? Lilah's gaze whipped through the living room as Sara hollered, "Net, get out here! Lilah and the kid are back!"

Lilah and the kid stood silently, shell-shocked from all that had happened this evening, as Nettie ran in from the kitchen. Wiping her hands on a dishtowel, the youngest Owens sister flashed her joyful smile. "Lilah!"

Black curls bouncing and arms flung wide, she raced to her sister. "I couldn't believe it when Sara told me you've been here almost the whole time I've been away. Shame on you for not calling my cell phone." She hugged tightly, her exuberance covering Lilah's motionlessness.

Releasing her sister, Nettie turned and thrust out her hand. "You must be Bree. I'm Nettie, Sara and Lilah's sane sister. Also the one who can cook. I hear you've been eating a lot of peanut butter sandwiches. How do you feel about fajitas?"

Bree stared at Nettie then mumbled, "I'm not hungry," and ran out of the room and up the stairs.

With a hand over her mouth, Nettie looked at Lilah. "Oh, my. That's the strongest reaction to Mexican food I've ever seen. Tough day?"

Lilah tried to smile. She tried to make a joke of it. She didn't think she could tolerate another frank conversation right now, or Nettie and Sara looking shocked when she told them the truth.

She just needed a little time to collect herself.

Trying to stay on an even keel, she shrugged unconcernedly. "You know kids. A couple cookies, one bad afternoon where they find out what a liar their guardian is, and their appetite is ruined." Her lips curved tremulously. "Gee, it's good to see you. Thanks for making dinner, I'm sure it'll be…delicious!" Sobbing the last word, she threw herself into her sister's arms, weeping as if the entire world were lost.

* * *

The night air smelled of clover.

Gus stood on the balcony outside his bedroom, his gaze set on the horizon, his mind locked on the past, the present, the future. The colors of the sunset were easier to separate and study than the tangle of his thoughts.

Discovering Lilah had had his child, that she'd been pregnant the last time he saw her before committing the acts that sent him to jail and then prison—that had shot a knife through his heart. And he couldn't seem to dislodge it.

He hadn't exaggerated when he'd told her it had taken him five years to be with another woman.

And even then, he'd thought of her. He'd been accused once of not committing. He'd been told he was "unavailable" and "hard on relationships." Comparisons did that. Reality had never stood a chance against his memories of her.

Dimly, he heard Elan's bedroom door close. At least there was one person who saw the current situation as something more than a tragic *Jerry Springer* episode. Elan didn't blame Gus, didn't seem to blame Lilah, either. He had merely asked a few basic questions, commented that Bree seemed pretty upset and that having three parents was better than being a foster kid. He thought he ought to tell that to Bree the next time he saw her.

Gus watched the fiery, sinking sun and wondered when he should attempt to contact Bree again, to try to speak with her. He didn't even want to think about Lilah right now. Couldn't. He kept thinking about how he would have felt if he'd never heard her lie about him to her friends, if instead they'd gone out the night of the prom, and he'd given her a ring…and she'd given him the news that she was carrying their baby.

The insistent ring of the phone pulled him from his reverie. He moved toward the phone, but the machine picked up before he could answer.

"Hello…this is Lilah. I'm sorry to call so late. Especially after… Oh, I'm just sorry to call, but Bree is missing, and I thought…I'm hoping… Is she at your place?" The quivering emotion in her tone made the hairs on Gus's neck stand on end. She began to speed up, the words tumbling over each other as she tried to speak past tears. "I thought she might have gone to see Elan? If you get this, would you call me? If she's not there, maybe Elan will have an idea of where she did go? I—"

"Lilah?" Gus snatched the phone and held it to his ear. He intended to tell her to calm down, begin from the beginning and tell him what happened. Instead, what he said was, "Hang tight. I'll be right over."

Earlier in the evening, Nettie had gone home to her family, although it had taken some persuading given her concern after listening to Lilah's story. She was back now, accompanied by her stepson, Colin, to hold Lilah's hand while Sara did the sheriff-ly thing and searched the area in her squad car.

Nettie was the one who answered the door when Gus knocked, and if he thought she would have forgotten him, he was mistaken.

"Gus Hoffman," she said, reaching for his arm and gently drawing him into the house. "It's good to see you. I've been meaning to look you up, welcome you back to town." She shook her head. "I'm sorry we're meeting again under these circumstances, but I'm glad you're here. For Lilah."

Gus was surprised. He'd never had too much to do with the youngest Owens sister—she'd been a couple grades behind him in school—but he recalled that she would unfailingly say hello when they crossed paths and that she'd always met his gaze directly, as she did now.

"Thank you," he said, wishing he could let go of the stiffness he still felt in the presence of Lilah's family.

In the presence of most anyone who'd known him as a boy.

Fitting in. That desire had been his motivator and his albatross most of his life. And to this day, Lilah was still the only person other than Elan with whom he'd fully accomplished his goal.

It occurred to him that he might be the one person here who understood a little bit of what Bree was going through.

"Any word?" he asked Nettie, his stomach pitching when her blue eyes darkened with worry.

"Sara and my husband, Chase, are out looking. Lilah's sick to her stomach and blaming herself. Bree actually climbed down the trellis outside her bedroom window. Lilah isn't sure exactly when she left, but we know she took Sara's old bike."

"She's not at our place." Gus spoke softly as Nettie led the way to the living room. "Doesn't mean she won't head there, though. Everybody is keeping an eye out. They have this number as well as my cell number."

Nettie nodded. When they entered the living room, Gus felt his heart lurch at the sight of Lilah, the girl whose smile had once lit the sky for him, sitting on the edge of the couch, hunched over and rocking herself as if the repetitive movement might dissipate some of the awful anxiety she was feeling.

"Lilah." Her name ached on his lips.

She looked up, pain and fear and need in her eyes, and for the first time in a dozen years there was no right or wrong clanging in Gus's head. No should or shouldn't or why that needed to be answered. There was only the two of them as they used to be—looking for love and doubting their ability to find it; and as they were now—older, still seeking, and not much wiser if the recent past was anything to go by.

Communicating her misery, Lilah's lower lip trembled. "She's gone, Gus. I let her down and she's gone." Her gaze wandered to the dark window and the now dark night. "She's all alone out there." Covering her face with her hands, she began to sob.

Gus did not hesitate. He joined her so swiftly that it later seemed he'd flown instead of walked. Lifting her to her feet, he pulled her into his arms. Lilah clung to the front of his shirt as he murmured assurances into her ear.

"She'll be fine, and you'll have plenty of chances to be there for her. We both will. We'll find her, baby. I promise."

If she heard him call her "baby," she didn't show it, except to cling harder.

Behind them, Nettie murmured something about tea and slipped from the room. Neither Gus nor Lilah heard her and neither knew that she had a smile on her face. She remembered the nights she'd sneaked to her bedroom window at midnight to watch them kiss in the shadows.

Pulling back slightly, Lilah backhanded the tears from her eyes. "Sara says I need to stay here, but I can't stand it." She shook her head. "I just can't! Nettie is here. I've got to go out and look for Bree myself."

Gus nodded. "I'll drive."

Lilah seemed to realize then that she was holding on to him. "Is it all right for you to come with me? Where's Elan? Do you need to—"

Gus put two fingers over her lips. "I'm right where I need to be. Let's not worry about anything except bringing our daughter home."

"Sara's searching all over town," Lilah said when she was seated in the passenger seat of Gus's Lexus. "But if Bree wants to hide, it could still be like looking for a needle in a haystack. And what if she rode her bike away from town?"

"Does she have any other relatives? Somewhere she might go? Be creative here, because she could be thinking about someone in another state. I once tried to run away to Florida."

He spoke lightly, but Lilah knew what he was really saying: Bree could have decided to ride the bike down the highway for all they knew. She began praying to God and to Grace and to her own parents, asking them all to surround Bree with their love.

"Grace was an only child and her parents were both gone. I know she had a big support system of friends. She left me a list of people she thought Bree should stay in touch with. Should we go back to the house and get it? Maybe Bree stopped somewhere to call one of them. Darn it! Why didn't I think of that right away?"

He covered her clenched fists with a palm. "No more shoulds or what ifs. We've had enough of those to last two lifetimes, I think."

Lilah looked at his hand, strong but gentle, then glanced at his profile. Gus's jaw was clenched with tension. She shook her head, unable to fathom why he was with her and why he was being so…warm. When he'd walked into Sara's living room, it had seemed so right that his motivation hadn't mattered.

Even now, she had no time to worry about why; she merely accepted that he was here, the way she knew she would have belonged with him if he'd been in a crisis. He was on loan tonight, and she was grateful. She would think of nothing beyond this moment and what she needed to do to find her daughter.

"Should we head back to the house?"

"Let's drive along the highway for a few miles before we do." He looked over. "Do you feel comfortable with that?"

Lilah nodded. Here, in the insulated world of his car, comforted by his touch, she could almost believe everything would be all right. Almost.

When his cell phone rang, it jolted them both.

Letting go of her hand, he reached for the small phone he'd clipped to his hip and flipped it open with one hand.

"Gus here." At first he listened quietly, then with anticipation he said, "Thanks, Loida, put him on. Elan, what did you remember, son?"

Lilah's heart began to pound, but with hope this time instead of abject fear. She wished Gus would say something, anything that would give her a clue about what Elan was telling him. Finally, he said, "No, you didn't say anything wrong. And it's good that you called. I'm proud of you. Tell Loida we'll call as soon as we know anything."

Lilah was ready to jump through his—closed— sunroof by the time he snapped his cell phone shut and turned to her.

"Elan remembered that he told Bree about the local cemetery."

"Cemetery. What about it?"

"There's a legend that suggests those who have lost loved ones will have success if they go there to contact the spirits of their ancestors. He said she told him a few days ago that her mother died and that she wished she could talk to her again, because there were some things she wanted to ask. Elan told her about the cemetery. I think it's worth a try." He raised a brow, waiting for her to make the decision.

"Let's do it."

The earliest gravesites in the Kalamoose cemetery dated back to 1855; the most recent had earth that had been freshly turned. Still, there was nothing modern or formal about the property, not even a gate to pass through. The lack of lighting made searching difficult, but the cemetery was small, so Lilah felt entitled to her misery when after walking every row of graves they saw no sign of Bree.

"Maybe we'd better go back to the house and make phone calls," she said. "If she did phone one of Grace's friends—"

"Shh." Gus held up a hand. He looked up at the sky. "Listen."

"I don't hear anything. I want to go back to the house and make calls. I'm getting really nervous again."

In lieu of answering, Gus motioned her to follow him and to be quiet.

They retraced the path they'd just taken, which frustrated Lilah. She wanted to get in the car, go back home and start making calls…or continue to comb the highway, looking for some sign that they were at least heading in the right direction. She felt ready to snap.

When they reached the end of one row of headstones, Gus continued walking until they came to a dilapidated gardener's shed that appeared not to be used for much of anything anymore, save as a shelter for spiders.

"We already checked that. It's locked," Lilah complained, but Gus put a finger to his lips.

Circling round to the back of the shed, he pointed to the structure. Lilah followed the direction of his finger, straining to see what he did in the dark. At first, she noted nothing of interest, but as her eyes adjusted to the shadows, she realized that one of the rotting wooden boards had broken completely loose. It was wide enough for a girl to slip through.

Gus put a finger to his ear, and Lilah listened closely. Soon she heard what he had—an intermittent whimper. Lilah gasped, hope hammering in her chest. She looked at Gus in question, amazed that he had heard it from so far away.

Shrugging with a small smile, he whispered, "Go get Bree. I'll call Sheriff Owens."

Chapter Fifteen

Gus swung the board on its rusty nail, lifting it so Lilah could squeeze through the opening. He'd already handed her the flashlight he'd brought from the car.

"Bree?" she called, shining the light through the filthy shed.

The circle of light landed on a thin girl who sat huddled in the corner, surrounded by rusty tools, her backpack at her feet. With her arms wrapped around her knees, Bree looked small and alone.

Lilah forgot the fears that had kept her from embracing Bree before. This time she didn't need an invitation.

Rushing over, she dropped to her knees, let go of the flashlight and took her daughter into her arms.

"Thank God you're safe. Everyone's been out looking for you." She held Bree so closely, the girl had to stretch out her legs so she wouldn't be squashed. "You scared me. Don't ever, ever even *think* about running way again. You got that? Not for any reason. I'll ground you till you're thirty."

Bree's arms stayed down, but she didn't pull away. "I wanted to talk to my mother," she said, sniffing back her tears. "That's why I left. Elan says the spirits of our ancestors stay with us and that people he knows come here to talk to them. But I talked and talked and nobody answered. I guess my mother…" Tears welled in her voice and she shook her head. "She didn't want to stay."

"Oh, Bree. Baby." Lilah took Bree's face in her hands and looked at her in the indirect glow of the flashlight. "That's not so. Your mother…Grace…she hasn't left you. She'll never leave, not completely. You can talk to her anytime you want, and you don't have to sit in a cemetery to do it. She's in here and here." Lilah touched Bree's head then placed her fingertips gently on Bree's chest. "When you want to talk to Grace, just sit for a while and listen to your heart. Every loving thing it tells you is coming from her."

"She told me my birth mother loved me," Bree said, her voice scratchy in the darkness. "She said that's why she…you gave me up."

It was a question. The hardest question, Lilah thought, a birth mother had to answer.

She plopped her bottom on the hard ground next to

Bree, sitting closely enough for their shoulders to touch. "I didn't give you up, Bree," she said slowly, searching for words that were accurate. "I made a plan for your life, because at that time I didn't even have a plan for my own. The first time I felt you kick inside me, I knew you'd be a firecracker of a kid, full of life, and I wanted you to have all the things I had no idea how to give you."

"Like clothes and a car and stuff like that?"

Lilah made a face. "Well, that was part of it. But in the end, no, that wasn't really the reason." She searched her daughter's face in the shadows. "I still can't give you great clothes, although I can teach you the fundamentals of smart thrift-store shopping. Don't count on the car, though, 'cause at the rate I'm going we may both be riding bikes before the end of the year. Where is your bike, anyway?"

"I ditched it in the bushes in case someone came looking for me."

"You're definitely grounded."

In the dim light, Lilah saw the beginning of a smile.

"Okay," she said, "here's the important stuff I couldn't give you. I couldn't give you security, the kind that comes from sensing the person who's taking care of you knows when and how to put you first. And discipline—" she shook her head "—I was hopeless at disciplining myself, much less a child, so stability and consistency were out, and you may not think so now, but that's really important to a kid, because without them you can grow up feeling like no one is running the show, and that can be nerve-racking."

Bree was listening and trying to understand. Lilah sighed, torn between frustration and resignation. How did you explain to a child something a lot of adults would have trouble understanding?

"I think this is a 'you had to be there' thing." Bree frowned.

"What?"

"My mom…" Bree hesitated a second, as if she was no longer sure what to call Grace when talking to Lilah. "Whenever she explained something she thought I wouldn't understand, she'd say, 'This is a you-had-to-be-there thing,' so I should just listen and remember what she said and not worry if I didn't get it right away."

"Well, your mom was brilliant," Lilah said, "and I hope you'll keep sharing her wisdom with me. 'Cause I may not be as good at this right off the bat as she was. I want to try, though, Bree. I want very, very much to try." She felt almost shy as she asked, "Will you give me—give us—a chance to be mother and daughter? I'm a lot older and a little smarter than I was when you were born, and I know that second chances don't always come along. I don't want to blow this one."

Once again, Lilah saw the whisper of Bree's smile, and this time it grew.

"I guess," her daughter agreed, apparently willing to try. "What about…him?"

"Him…Gus?" At Bree's shy, nervous nod, Lilah said, "Gus was the first person I called when I realized you were missing. He was still pretty upset with me, but he didn't ask any questions. Just jumped in the car and said, 'We'll find her.' 'Our daughter'—that's what he called you."

Bree liked that. She wrestled with a smile.

"Gus wasn't ready to be a dad when he was a teenager." Lilah decided to just touch on that topic for the time being. "He's ready now. Whatever happens between him and me, he wants to be your father, and I think he's going to be a really great one."

Bree thought it over. "Will me and Elan be, like, brother and sister?"

"Yeah, like that."

"Okay, I guess. I'm pretty hungry," she said, starting a new topic and making Lilah shake her head at the lack of transition.

"There are fajitas left at the house."

"Okay."

Lilah retrieved the flashlight and they stood, picking their way around rusty tools and an ominous number of spiderwebs.

Just as they reached the loose board that was their exit, Bree asked, "So were you and Gus like in love or something? 'Cause you still act really doofus around him."

Lilah smacked her forehead on the shed. Hard.

The shadows on the ceiling were a comfort.

Moon glow and tree leaves patterned the room, and as Lilah lay in bed, staring up, she marveled at how appealing her old bedroom seemed tonight. With fewer shadows in her life, she could better appreciate the ones decorating her walls.

For the first time in years, she had cleared the air and cleared her conscious along with it. Her sisters now knew about Bree and about Gus…although Nettie, it turned out, had known about her and Gus back in high school. The fact that she'd kept mum was typically Nettie. The fact that this infuriated Sara was typically Sara.

It would take time, of course, for Bree to truly trust her, but Lilah was determined to give her daughter every reason to believe in the bond they were forming.

Even with the challenges she knew they'd face, Lilah felt lighter and happier than she had in ages. There was only one shadow left. One part of her life that still felt unfinished. Gus had gone home after making sure she and Bree were okay.

Rolling onto her side, Lilah drew her knees to her chest, thoughts of Gus disturbing the peace she had found.

Now that the crisis was over, she tried to remember what he'd said, how he'd touched her. Had he called her "baby" at one point, or was her mind playing tricks?

She knew it was wrong to think about him, wrong to try to analyze all he'd said and done. The important thing was that he and Bree develop a healthy relationship, and if she had to stay out of it to ensure less strife, then that's what she had to do.

Throwing off the even the lightest of her covers, she swung her bare legs to the floor and sat hunched on the edge of the bed. She and Gus would have to work out visitation. It was highly possible that she would stay in Kalamoose or nearby, to give Bree the benefit of two parents.

That meant she and Gus would see each other frequently. She made no assumptions about continuing a romantic relationship. They both had a lot on their plates now.

"I need a shower," she muttered. "I'm going to need a lot of very long and *very* cold showers."

Reaching for her watch on the nightstand, she squinted, trying to read the face in the moonlight. 12:05 a.m. Groaning softly, she replaced the watch and pitched the notion of commencing her shower marathon right now; she didn't want to risk waking anyone.

Deciding that raiding Sara's chocolate stash would provide the same distraction as a cold shower and taste a whole lot better, she pushed off the bed, mentally perusing the different candy varieties Sara had in the basket she kept atop the fridge.

She was going to have to find a new career anyway; she was a lousy actress, really. Struggling all day to get an under-five role on a soap opera and then waiting tables all night was no way to raise a child; what would a few candy-induced pounds matter? If it kept her mind off Gus, she'd eat the whole damn basket.

Rising, she headed toward the door. She was just picturing biting into a chocolate-covered nougat with caramel oozing out when she heard a *ping* on her window. The unexpectedness of it made her jump.

Turning toward the sound, she waited, wondering if it had been a bird or some other flying thing connecting with the glass.

The next noise she heard sounded more like splattering rocks.

Racing to the window, she connected with the edge of the bed frame, grabbed her smarting ankle and hopped on one foot while swearing as softly as she could.

When the initial pain died down, she limped to the window and looked out.

Nothing. Nothing but familiar shapes in shades of gray and black. Her car…Sara's…the tree Sara fell out of when she was fourteen and set up surveillance in the front yard….

Disappointment hurt more than her ankle.

Yeah. Well, real bright, Lilah. What are you, anyway, fifteen? Your ex-boyfriend is going to throw rocks at your window? Unlikely at this juncture.

She shook her head. Obviously, it would take more than nougat to get her mind off of Gus. She considered the package of Mallomars and half-gallon of Moose Tracks she'd spied in the freezer. It was a start.

About to turn away, she noticed a movement in the tree where the trunk spread into branches. She watched for several seconds then gasped and raced out the bedroom door and down the stairs, sore ankle ignored.

When she reached the kitchen, she wrestled with the

safety locks on the door. "Damn it, Sara, get a guard dog!" Wrenching the last lock free, she flung open the door and ran into the night.

She didn't stop running until she was standing beneath the tree, looking up, positive about what she had seen.

"What are you doing?" she asked the man in the branches.

Startled, he lost his footing, which made the limbs shake. He swore. When he'd restabilized, he looked down to chastise, "It is not a good idea to surprise a man in a tree, Lilah. It is particularly unhealthy when you do it in the middle of the night."

"You're lecturing me? You're the one stuck in a tree."

"I'm not stuck." To prove it, Gus began to pick his way down the limbs.

"What were you trying to do up there, exactly?"

"I was trying to get higher," he said, continuing the descent.

"Higher? Have you been smoking something you shouldn't? Because this behavior seems a little—"

He interrupted by jumping past the lowest branches and landing in front of her. Glaring as effectively as a man could glare in the dark, he asked, "Do we have to have this part of the conversation?"

Lilah tried to calm the sweet swell of anticipation that came from seeing him again—in the dark, in a tree… however. The skip-thud-skip of her heart told her they were in dangerous territory. He would leave again tonight, and when he did, there wouldn't be enough sugar in all of North Dakota to dull the pain. "Are we going to have a conversation?"

"I didn't drive out here in the middle of the night to throw rocks at your window for old times' sake. Well, partly for old times' sake." The moon lit up his smile.

"Gus. I'm sure this is all…innocent and everything, but—"

"It's not innocent at all. Although I do intend for my visit to include a little bit of 'everything.'"

It might have been the effect of straining to see someone in the dark, but Lilah began to feel dizzy.

Gus frowned at her. "I'm going to say what I came to say whether you want to hear it or not. But it would be nice to know before I pour my heart out whether my climbing a tree for you comes as a…not unpleasant surprise."

Lilah was so giddy now, her poor brain had to work hard to latch on to his words. "Are you going to pour your heart out?"

"Yes, I am."

"And you're still single?"

"Yes, of course. So, are you glad to see me?"

The dizziness intensified. "What's that?"

She heard a sound not unlike the gnashing of teeth.

"I said, are you glad to see me, *for God's sake, Lilah?*"

"Shh. Yes." She whispered to counter the fact that he'd spoken loudly enough to wake the house. "I'm glad you're here, and I'm very glad you're going to pour your heart out. Not that you have to. We could just…hang out. I mean, unless you want to talk tonight. Then—"

Obviously he felt the only way to stop her nervous babble was to kiss her.

Hauling her into his arms, he lowered his head and met her mouth with a hunger that had waited too long to be easily satisfied.

Lilah tried to notice everything—the hand on her back pressing her ever closer...the thighs grazing hers...the palm cupping her head and holding her as though he feared she might disappear if he let go. The lips that clung so hungrily.

The kiss started hard then turned soft and searching.

She wound her arms around his neck. They had more questions than answers right now, but Lilah would not let that stop her from allowing her heart to flow through her fingertips as she pushed them into the hair at his nape. She held back nothing when she ran her tongue over his lips and felt her whole body quake with the revelation that he could still make her feel more than any other man ever had, ever would.

They might have stayed entwined until dawn, kissing, tasting, recapturing all they'd lost for so long had Gus not had the presence to pull his head back and look at her.

"I'm not here for a night. Or to hang out. I want a lot more than that." He sounded like someone who'd run a ten-mile race. "I wish I'd been there for everything you've gone through. If I'd known... If I hadn't been such a moron...hadn't been in jail...I *would* have been there. I'd like to throttle myself for letting you go through everything you did alone."

Lilah shook her head. "I wish I could do so many things over again, too. But I would never take back the experience of Bree."

Untangling one arm from around him, she laid her palm against his cheek, pressing gently, feeling the warmth and the roughness and thinking it was perfect.

"What I wish," she whispered, not because she was afraid of being overheard this time, but because she feared her voice might crack if she raised it, "is that I'd told my friends I loved you long before that day in high school. I wish we'd never hidden a thing. I wish I hadn't been so hungry to have the whole world love me that I destroyed the only love that really mattered. Can you honestly forgive me, Gus? I know you're here, but…" Worry made her bite her lip.

"Don't do that." He shook his head, his voice soft, his eyes even softer. With one gentle finger he traced her lower lip. "I've told you and told you. You'll wear down your lips that way. And they drive me crazy just as they are."

"You can't wear down your lips," she smiled.

"You can't wear down my love, either."

Shifting his hand to cup her jaw, he made sure she was looking straight at him when he said, "I can let go of the pains, Lilah, both of them—the one I felt and the one I caused. What I can't let go of and don't ever want to let go of is how it feels to be loved by you. When we're not together, my soul keeps looking for its missing piece."

He brushed back her hair, not because it needed it,

but because he wanted to touch, to rediscover the parts of her he'd missed all these years.

"I'm not very good at love. But I'll listen better, try to make fewer mistakes. And when you make mistakes, I promise to forgive more easily."

"Gus, Gus," she murmured, shaking her head and kissing him to stem the flow of promises. "You sound like you're auditioning," she told him lovingly as she stood back. "You don't have to, not for me. Not ever for me."

"Being your husband is a role I'll audition for every day for the rest of my life until you say yes."

Lilah was so busy trying thinking up exactly the right way to tell him she would never ever, ever again take his love for granted that it took a few seconds to realize he'd proposed. When she got it, she gasped, squealed and then jumped into his arms. This time she rained kisses all over his face.

"For Pete's sake, stop kissing, and say yes, already! And get inside before people start calling the office to report a disturbance."

Keeping their arms around each other, Gus and Lilah pulled apart enough to look at the upper-floor window from which Sara and Bree delightedly spied.

"Can we live at his house?" Bree called down.

Lilah felt herself blush. She looked at Gus. "We're definitely going to need to talk to her and Elan about all this."

Sara put an arm around Bree. "Come on, kid." To the couple below, she called, "Now that we're awake, we're going to make pancakes, if anyone is interested."

Gus and Lilah watched as the duo left the window and lights clicked on inside the house.

"We made a spectacle of ourselves," Lilah murmured, feeling less awful than she probably should have.

"Why break a twelve-year tradition?" Gus asked. Searching her face, he said, "You willing to try again, Lilah Owens?"

"To try and to keep trying," she nodded, "until we get it right."

"Could take a long time," he cautioned.

"With our track record?" A smile brightened her face. "My love, this could take a lifetime."

* * * * *

Look for award-winning author,
Wendy Warren's next book
THE BABY BARGAIN
the fourth installment in the
new Special Edition continuity
LOGAN'S LEGACY REVISITED
On sale April 2007,
wherever Silhouette Books are sold.

Turn the page for a sneak preview of
IF I'D NEVER KNOWN YOUR LOVE
by
Georgia Bockoven

From the brand-new series
Harlequin Everlasting Love
Every great love has a story to tell.™

One year, five months and four days missing

There's no way for you to know this, Evan, but I haven't written to you for a few months. Actually, it's been almost a year. I had a hard time picking up a pen once more after we paid the second ransom and then received a letter saying it wasn't enough. I was so sure you were coming home that I took the kids along to Bogotá so they could fly home with you and me, something I swore I'd never do. I've fallen in love with Colombia and the people who've opened their hearts to me. But fear is a constant companion when I'm there. I won't ever expose our children to that kind of danger again.

I'm at a loss over what to do anymore, Evan. I've begged and pleaded and thrown temper tantrums with every official I can corner both here and at home. They've been incredibly tolerant and understanding, but in the end as ineffectual as the rest of us.

I try to imagine what your life is like now, what you do every day, what you're wearing, what you eat. I want to believe that the people who have you are misguided yet kind, that they treat you well. It's how I survive day to day. To think of you being mistreated hurts too much. If I picture you locked away somewhere and suffering, a weight descends on me that makes it almost impossible to get out of bed in the morning.

Your captors surely know you by now. They have to recognize what a good man you are. I imagine you working with their children, telling them that you have children, too, showing them the pictures you carry in your wallet. Can't the men who have you understand how much your children miss you? How can it not matter to them?

How can they keep you away from us all this time? Over and over, we've done what they asked. Are they oblivious to the depth of their cruelty? What kind of people are they that they don't care?

I used to keep a calendar beside our bed next to the peach rose you picked for me before you left. Every night I marked another day, counting how many you'd been gone. I don't do that any longer. I don't want to be reminded of all the days we'll never get back.

When I can't sleep at night, I tell you about my day. I imagine you hearing me and smiling over the details that make up my life now. I never tell you how defeated I feel at moments or how hard I work to hide it from everyone for fear they will see it as a reason to stop believing you are coming home to us.

And I couldn't tell you about the lump I found in my breast and how difficult it was going through all the tests without you here to lean on. The lump was benign—the process reaching that diagnosis utterly terrifying. I couldn't stop thinking about what would happen to Shelly and Jason if something happened to me.

We need you to come home.

I'm worn down with missing you.

I'm going to read this tomorrow and will probably tear it up or burn it in the fireplace. I don't want you to get the idea I ever doubted what I was doing to free you or thought the work a burden. I would gladly spend the rest of my life at it, even if, in the end, we only had one day together.

You are my life, Evan.

I will love you forever.

* * * * *

*Don't miss this deeply moving
Harlequin Everlasting Love story
about a woman's struggle to bring
back her kidnapped husband from Colombia
and her turmoil over whether to let go, finally,
and welcome another man into her life.
IF I'D NEVER KNOWN YOUR LOVE
by Georgia Bockoven
is available March 27, 2007.*

*And also look for
THE NIGHT WE MET
by Tara Taylor Quinn,
a story about finding love
when you least expect it.*

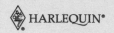

presents a brand-new trilogy by

PATRICIA THAYER

Three sisters come home to wed.

In April don't miss

Raising the Rancher's Family,

followed by

The Sheriff's Pregnant Wife,

on sale May 2007,

and

A Mother for the Tycoon's Child,

on sale June 2007.

From *New York Times* bestselling author

SHERRYL WOODS

The Sweet Magnolias

 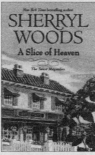 

February 2007 **March 2007** **April 2007**

SAVE $1.⁰⁰ off the purchase price of any book in *The Sweet Magnolias* trilogy.

Offer valid from February 1, 2007 to April 30, 2007. Redeemable at participating retail outlets. Limit one coupon per purchase.

52607602

Canadian Retailers: Harlequin Enterprises Limited will pay the face value of this coupon plus 10.25¢ if submitted by customer for this product only. Any other use constitutes fraud. Coupon is nonassignable. Void if taxed, prohibited or restricted by law. Consumer must pay any government taxes. Void if copied. Nielson Clearing House ("NCH") customers submit coupons and proof of sales to: Harlequin Enterprises Limited, P.O. Box 3000, Saint John, N.B. E2L 4L3, Canada. Non-NCH retailer—for reimbursement submit coupons and proof of sales directly to: Harlequin Enterprises Limited, Retail Marketing Department, 225 Duncan Mill Rd., Don Mills, Ontario M3B 3K9, Canada.

U.S. Retailers: Harlequin Enterprises Limited will pay the face value of this coupon plus 8¢ if submitted by customer for this product only. Any other use constitutes fraud. Coupon is nonassignable. Void if taxed, prohibited or restricted by law. Consumer must pay any government taxes. Void if copied. For reimbursement submit coupons and proof of sales directly to: Harlequin Enterprises Limited, P.O. Box 880478, El Paso, TX 88588-0478, U.S.A. Cash value 1/100 cents.

5 65373 00076 2 (8100) 0 11383

MSWSMT07

REQUEST YOUR FREE BOOKS!
2 FREE NOVELS PLUS 2 FREE GIFTS!

SPECIAL EDITION®
Life, Love and Family!

SSE07

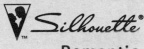

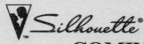